The Tale of Don l'Orignal

The Tale of Don l'Orignal

Antonine Maillet

translated by Barbara Godard

Clarke, Irwin & Company Limited
Toronto/Vancouver

Canadian Cataloguing in Publication Data

Maillet, Antonine, 1929 —
(Don l'Orignal. English)
The tale of Don l'Orignal

Translation of Don l'Orignal.

ISBN 0-7720-1216-4

I. Title. II. Title: Don l'Orignal. English.

PS8526.A54D613   843'.5'4   C78-001515-0
PQ3919.2.M26D613

First published in French by Les Editions Leméac Inc.
under the title *Don l'Orignal*. French edition © 1972 by
Les Editions Leméac Inc.

Printed in Canada

The Tale of Don l'Orignal

Chapter One

Concerning the strange birth of a little island destined to be great.

On the shores of the country right next to yours where I still live, in front of a village whose name I've forgotten how to spell, there arose one fine morning in the middle of the ocean a sort of yellow blob that looked just like a golden whale.

Such a phenomenon had never occurred before so close to their country. As soon as the alarm was given the mainlanders hurried to the shore and spent the morning there deep in contemplation. Then at noon, the mayor shivered, tossed her feathered bun, and proclaimed her profoundest thoughts to the assembled town.

"It's an island of hay," she said.

The barber, the milliner, the merchant, the school-master, the banker, the nursing sister and the older children instantly relaxed, and their rapture faded away.

"It's only an island," passed from mouth to mouth, "an island of hay."

And each returned to his business or way of life, leaving the island of hay to the sea that had brought it into the world.

However, oceans that give birth to islands don't take them back until they've done their time and fulfilled their destiny, gambolling and splashing about, and spattering nearby shores too if they don't watch out. This is what the island of hay did. Its neighbours had underestimated how deep and solid it was.

Thus the people of the mainland turned their eyes and attention away from the island, too eager to plant, hoe, pick, gather, produce and market to concern themselves with a tiny little island of hay. And so it was able to shoot up and flower in peace, ignored and forsaken by all continents.

But one night, the lighthouse keeper directed his search-light at the island and felt something crawl under his shirt. In the hay at the end of his spyglass he had just caught sight of a whole species of jumping, flying, biting creatures on feet, strangely resembling a population of fleas. The island of hay was inhabited, occupied by the most execrable and contagious race that any civilized neighbour (made respectable by centuries of culture) could ever have feared.

The island of hay was an island of fleas.

The keeper lost no time. He went down the one hundred and thirty-two steps of the lighthouse without counting. Short of breath, his faith shaken, he roused the sleeping village from the repose of the just. In less than an hour, the best minds of the town (cultivated by the mayor, barber, milliner, merchant, schoolmaster, banker and nursing sister) surrounded the breathless, pale face of the keeper. And there in the square, on a starless and moonless night, the inhabitants of the mainland learned that the island of hay was an island of fleas. And they resolved, that night, to destroy it.

To anyone who has never set his mind to such a task, the destruction of an island might seem like child's play, just a matter of sending it back where it came from—in this case to the bottom of the sea. Since it had already grown too big for a single kick or blow to sink it, the barber proposed to cut it first into little pieces, then give each district of the town its slice of island to set upon and finish off. The milliner found this method shameful and pernicious and suggested instead a powerful insecticide capable of reducing the very roots of life to cinders, drying up the island so it would float away over foreign seas and run aground some day at the other end of the world. The merchant expressed the opinion that they should sell it to a neighbouring country and, to this end, at once began to proclaim the discovery of a new world.

"Terra incognita," uttered the schoolmaster.

But the mayor remained deaf to all this considered advice, continuing to gnaw on the lace of her high collar.

The banker proposed that they destroy the fleas but save the island, since all empty land is valuable real estate which one could exploit or inhabit. The nursing sister fell in with this position, on the condition, however, that the fleas not be harmed.

Meanwhile, seeing that the deliberations were going on so long (many suns could have risen and set since the discovery of the island and many moons since the finding of the fleas), the keeper had climbed back up the one hundred and thirty-two steps of his lighthouse. And it was there, at the point where sky, land and water meet, that he saw the sun rise one fine day on the extraordinary and unforeseeable event which is the subject of this very true story. Flea Island was peopled with men, women, children, dogs, cats and rabbits. An entire species had landed on the island or had risen up through the hay or had somehow evolved from the fleas. However it happened, a people had been born, had built their shacks and dug wells there. They were there, standing upright, feet dug into the soft soil of the island, chests thrust forward and brows lashed by the four winds.

Chapter Two

Concerning the kingdom of Flea Island where, in those days, reigned the noble and formidable Don l'Orignal.

The little island rapidly grew in importance. For nothing is peopled as quickly as an isolated, barren land, neglected by everyone, since good lands remain by right the lot of the upper class, that uncommon and scattered species so scrupulously called the elite. Thus, in less time than it would take to establish a respectable family on the firm soil of the mainland, the soft soil of the island had engendered a nation.

The citizens of the mainland never knew how life had been organized over there, when a government had been formed or laws established. But they learned from the keeper that a coronation had certainly taken place, since Flea Island had become a kingdom. Indeed, every evening the lighthouse could follow the ceremony taking place around a shack slightly taller than the others. In front of this shack a horned colossos, bearded and hairy, was enthroned on a stump.

Don l'Orignal wore fake horns at the four corners of his fur hat just to show that he was king. But the beard and the hair were his own. He put buckskin on his shoulders and pigskin boots on his feet. Dressed in this manner, Don l'Orignal ruled over Flea Island as king and over his house as the father of an only son. This son almost never slept under his father's roof. Not that Don l'Orignal had tyrannized his son, the hardy and fearless knight, Noume, but the valorous Noume had many chicks to pluck those nights.

The inhabitants of Flea Island needed only to cross half an ocean to land on the mainland, and, for this reason, the mainland felt constantly threatened.

"Their island looks like a soldier's boot," said the barber.

"Like a battleship," said the milliner.

But neither the milliner nor the barber had ever seen a war. They only talked about it because they had read the history of the Boer War which sat on the top shelf of the municipal library. For three and a half months they had discussed the book, arguing about everything—the style, the ideas, the thesis, the language, the style, the thesis, the chapter divisions, the composition, the ideas, the language, the words—agreeing on only one point: the negroes were barbarians who had to be put in their place.

"One day they'll have to be put in their place," said the mayor to the lighthouse keeper, one night when she had voluntarily climbed up to keep watch for a short time.

Faced with this quiet resolution, such as had won Napoleon his empire in Europe, the keeper bared his four fangs like a good watchdog, ready to devour the whole island at a single word from his legitimate sovereign. However, that night the mayor said no more, keeping all these things in her heart.

Chapter Three

Concerning the mayor's amazing dream and the great resolution which ensued.

The mayor held the highest rank in the civil hierarchy and consequently recognized, along with the entire municipality, that she deserved the greatest respect. Ladies curtsied to her, men bowed as she passed and the town's chief officials always repeated after her that the good operation of a state rests on the wise government of one individual. For nearly a generation the mayor had assured this wise government, basing it on two unbeatable political principles: "Good blood never lies," and, "The will of woman is the will of God." So in twenty-eight years the mayor had never failed to fall asleep as soon as her head touched the pillow.

Now it happened that the appearance of an island of hay, first occupied by fleas, then peopled by an ambiguous species, troubled her sleep. This was the night, the critical night just referred to, that she spent behind the lighthouse windows.

For twenty-eight years as a politician and fifty-eight years as a woman the mayor had conducted herself according to the most sound and lofty principles. Now, following in the footsteps of Joan of Arc, Pauline and Athaliah, she experienced that glorious and terrifying thing, a prophetic dream.

That night, after a hearty supper of pâté de foie gras and cheese cake, the mayor had a strange and upsetting vision. Powerless, she had witnessed the clash of two opposed armies, rising up unexpectedly from her inkwell and desk lamp. Thousands of tiny wooden soldiers confronted each other on the table, brandishing pencils, rulers, pens, hairpins and toothbrushes. They aimed, struck and fired at each other without a word being spoken in either camp. Then one

7

general jumped to the ground and his whole army followed him like Panurge's sheep, drawing the enemy along in pursuit until they drew up into battle line again. And the war continued on the carpet.

The army on the right was much better disciplined. It advanced in good battle formation with standard aloft, visors lowered, eyes aflame. At its head marched the leader, draped in a long barber's smock. In contrast, the army on the left looked like a gang of Carthaginian mercenaries, pushing, swearing, fighting among themselves, tripping and thumbing their noses at each other.

Without quite knowing how the change came about, the mayor realized, in less time than it takes to say it, that the army had grown, that it was invading the whole room, making the walls crack, spreading out into the village, into the fields, along the shoreline, flooding the land and water with its war-like wrath. The world was now a vast battlefield strewn with cannons, cannonballs, the dead, the half-dead, the not-so-dead, the dead more or less in the process of breathing their last.

Suddenly, separating himself from this very gloomy picture, a soldier rose up like a badly embalmed Lazarus. He came straight towards the mayor, who was frozen behind the table. Slowly, as if performing a sacred ritual, he tightened the elastic band of his slingshot and let fly a bean as big as a flea at the mayor's left temple. Surprise jolted her awake and she realized she had been dreaming. She wiped her brow with her hand and a fly took wing.

The mayor didn't sleep any more that night. She made her way straight to the lighthouse and glued her eyes to the lens of the spyglass for the rest of the night. Little by little the idea innocently began to grow that her dream might have been prophetic. But unlike Pharoah, she didn't search the state prisons for a poor Joseph to interpret it. She considered herself sufficiently capable of having the vision and also unravelling its meaning. For the moment, the essential thing was to diagnose the danger, assess her strengths and those of the enemy. The rest would follow as an appetite comes with eating. After all, desperate ills require desperate remedies, she said to herself, while she said aloud to the keeper, "They must be put in their place."

But what would this place be? And by what means should they be put there? The mayor did not reveal the secrets of her heart that night, but resolutely went back down the one hundred and thirty-two steps of the tower.

Chapter Four

Concerning the loyal and faithful subjects of Don l'Orignal, and their illustrious origin.

Since the death of Don l'Orignal's wife (he cried so hard he nearly bust half the half-a-gut he still had left), the first lady of the court in the kingdom of Flea Island was La Sagouine, faithless companion of Michel-Archange, the king's armour bearer. This brave squire—a giant by nature and a savage by choice—had gone to look for his wife in the home of one of the most famous men in the kingdom, Jos à Pit à Boy à Thomas Picoté Viens-que-je-t'arrache.

This Jos à Pit à Boy, to call him by his first name, was a fiery man to whom were attributed the most illustrious deeds ever dreamed of by valiant knights. The tale was told on the island of the time when, still a child, he had shut up his stepmother, a flabby shrew six feet tall, in an abandoned potato cellar. The frightful stepmother roused the country with her cries, but to all her would-be rescuers, our hero candidly replied that he and his brothers had slit a pig's throat while their father was away. It would not die and was up to its old tricks down in the cellar. Nevertheless, after the third day of the pig's death-struggle, the Order of the Suspender gathered about Don Gros-Ventre the first, illustrious father of the present king, and the royal assembly decided to send a scout to the cellar of the Viens-que-je-t'arrache. The king's army freed the old woman and dragged Jos à Pit before His Highness, who decided to hand the case over to the paternal justice of Pit à Boy à Thomas Picoté. When he returned from smelt fishing and learned of the glorious feat of his son, the patriarch cuffed him on the ear and laughed heartily, "Next time, gag er up, too, cause she's a bitch who's always gettin round us, either with er big mouth or . . ."

But the rest of the sentence was swept away by a slap from the tender woman who had not left all her strength in the cellar and had a few accounts to settle with the family that had taken her for wife and mother.

It is from this family that La Sagouine sprang, as from Jupiter's thigh. The daughter of Jos à Pit à Boy à Thomas Picoté Viens-que-je-t'arrache bore all the virtues of her ancestors: boldness, pluck, voice, keen eye, craftiness, and absolute queenly scorn for all who claimed to be of a lineage superior to hers. But among her own folk, she had secrets from nobody and refused no one. At the time of the great and glorious feats related in this story, this Sagouine reigned as honourable mistress over all Flea Island.

Second in rank was La Sainte, a retiring woman if ever there was one, who preferred to keep for herself and God all the intimate treasures with which her rival La Sagouine was so lavish. The face she showed to the jovial and lively Flea Islanders was the dry, yellow one of an ascetic who can't digest her fodder and won't forgive the rest of mankind for its good digestion.

All this virtue, however, didn't stop La Sainte from giving birth to a gallant child, a son by the name of Citrouille, who would change the face of his island when he attained manhood. But for the moment, Citrouille grew in simplicity and tenderness, ever since the day when, fishing for oysters on foreign shores, he had seen the beautiful Adeline sunbathing.

As the lover Citrouille pined away, Noume, whose liege man he was, gained in strength and boldness. This champion already had many deeds to his credit. Son and grandson of kings, Noume showed a subtle mind and conquering spirit. He never left his island without leaving all hearts aflame or in ashes in his wake. This new Alexander knew better then all his forebears how to tame recalcitrant mares. And the mares were grateful to him.

Besides Citrouille, the royal Noume had a faithful companion in his old fencing-master, the valorous and invulnerable Michel-Archange who was his father's squire and husband of Lady Sagouine. This Archange had received his name after his famous battle with a hell-hound, the late Sam Amateur, who had come from beyond the grave to disturb the peace of the land. One day I shall tell you of that struggle with the angel which almost compromised Flea Island's well-being. But other glorious feats awaited our hero who stood there, like a new Don Quixote, ready to avenge the weak, redress wrongs, sow the wind to reap the whirlwind, rob Peter to pay Paul, make omelettes without breaking eggs, do what must be done, come what may. And above everything, the great maxim of Michel-Archange, the king's squire, was written in gold letters on the family coat of arms: "As the wine is poured, so must we drink."

Then to enliven this group of courageous men, there lived on Flea Island a princess of the blood royal, answering to the name of La Cruche. She had forfeited her rights because of some obscure family transgression (the nature of which had best be kept secret) handed down from mother to daughter. However, this beauty had not lost her powers, which rivalled those of the lord, Don l'Orignal, among the knights and bums of the island.

At the time of the events which our tale relates, this was the rank of the principal actors in the great drama that would bring Flea Island into the history of the world.

Chapter Five

Concerning the conversation the Flea Islanders had one day around a keg of molasses.

One day, La Sagouine reported to the king of her island with her eyes glowering and her claws showing.

"Well?" she said.

And the whole assembly grew silent. Michel-Archange and Citrouille looked down at the ground and the bums stared at the sky. On this day it was all pocked with tiny clouds that looked like many ancient gods come there to applaud the entertaining spectacle which was about to unfold below.

Then Michel-Archange shook the mane covering his eyes and began this beautiful speech, which deserves to be told in full.

"That's how she be, then. There we was, all four of us, me, the bums and Citrouille. We beached the dory and cast anchor. Then we started climbin the rock on all fours, no sweat. First to see us was the keeper. I know that cause just as we's passin under his tower the sonuvabitch lets go his lamp and one of his 'what the hells.' So we took off. Nobody seen us in the streets. We slips behind them barns and fish sheds. Slips so good one of the bums leaves three parts of his shirt caught in a window. Then we goes off to the store. We brushes our duds, straightens our backs, opens up the door and there's the four of us facin the mayor, the milliner, the barber, the banker and the storeman hidin behind the counter. Seems like the lighthouse keeper didn't waste no time. All them bigwigs in the country was lyin waitin fer us like a ecumulical council."

"Skunks," said La Sagouine.

"Pigs," added La Sainte.

But neither of these noble beasts was sufficient to incarnate the women's rage at the enemy's base treachery. And the noble Sagouine spat on the ground three times.

Then they learned how the merchant, under the intimidating eye of the mayor and her escort, had refused to sell a keg of molasses to the delegation from Flea Island.

"And the fire took, first just glowin embers, pfff pfft . . . then a real good forest fire, pshpshpsh! Before ya knows it, the place'd burned down. Pfffftpfft . . . pshpshpsh! We opens our eyes and there's nobody there but me, the bums and Citrouille. Everybody'd beat the hell outa there."

"Cept the storeman, scared stiff as a board," added a bum.

"So there ya got it," concluded Archange.

At this strategic moment in the discussion, Don l'Orignal stretched out his left leg, raised an eyebrow, and snorted. Then, lifting his sceptre shaped like a spruce branch up to the sun to impose silence, he solemnly uttered, "God-almightyhellfire!"

And all the assembled people understood by this speech from the throne that the die was cast.

So they threw themselves body and soul into an illuminating debate worthy of the most august House of Commons. Hair stood on end, feet beat the ground and fists drew fantastic arabesques in the sky.

"First of all the mayor," said La Sagouine, "then the milliner, then the barber, then the storekeeper . . ."

"Then it's all them pretty girls in the village."

"Don't touch them girls. Us men'll look after the milliners and the barbers ourselves. Leave them pretty girls fer Citrouille."

Citrouille leaped at Michel-Archange, but Don l'Orignal raised his sceptre and separated them.

"No fightin while the sun's up."

"Bejeezus! That got him! Just maybe I said somethin true?"

"These days," l'Orignal began again, "anythin a man can stuff into his thick skull he can bury in his guts."

"Still ya gotta see if a guy that's always sneakin round that country over there's got any guts."

"Everybody has his day, Michel-Archange. I remember yers. That happened on this side of the fence."

"Damn right. On this here side of the fence. I walk in my own shit, lemme tell ya, not in other people's."

"Cause their shit don't stink so much," ventured Citrouille.

"Not when they stuff it down yer mug. Tarnation!"

La Sagouine stood up then, shook her rump and launched her most fiercesome challenge at the sky.

"I'm gonna get to the bottom on it, I'm tellin ya. I'm gonna learn the long and the short on it."

"Don't trust nobody."

"Holy bread ain't fer slaves."

"Ain't a place in the sun fer everybody."

"Bejeezus!"

"Prrrt!"

"That's what makes big shots."

"Bad weeds grows fast."

"Mary Mother of God fer Christ sake."

"Tarnation!"

"Every pot's got his cover."

"The only pot you'll cover's the one ya sits on."

"Jeezus Christ Godalmighty, shut up!"

"Like they says, he who gives to the Lord lends to the poor."

"Yeah!"

"Shut up!"

"Bejeezus!"

"Cheep - cheep! Devil's pointed chin, silver mouth, nose, quack - quack . . ."

"Godalmightyhellfire!"

Thus ended the first political skirmish which opposed Flea Island to the mainland. The Estates-General dispersed, happy to have done their duty in saving the nation.

Chapter Six

Concerning the triumphal return of Noume, Don l'Orignal's son, and his heroic deeds.

One morning when the bums were pumping their accordions or plucking the loosened strings of their guitars, the hay on Flea Island suddenly quivered to an unfamiliar sound. Far away through the fog a schooner sent its message of hope.

In less than five minutes, all of Flea Island had climbed to the top of all the posts in the kingdom. With their legs wound twice around these poles and their hands held as visors, they watched the masts silhouetted against the horizon.

Suddenly, a little Flea man no taller than a boot cried out from his post that he saw white smoke to the east.

"Smoke! Smoke!"

And everybody jumped into the hay and ran down to the shore.

Now the schooner was completely visible. It smiled with all its sails and rocked its hull, swollen with the most beautiful cod from the Grand Banks. At the prow of this elegant vessel our hero first appeared to his people, massed on the shore.

"Ahoy! Ahoy!" called the schooner.

And Flea Island replied, "Noume!"

When the ship drew alongside the quai facing the village, one man was missing, for Don l'Orignal's son had not waited for customs or naval formalities to jump ashore. For an instant the tip of a dune had tickled his schooner, and he had taken advantage of this, and of a very brief but opportune moment of distraction on the part of his captain.

It was Lady Sagouine who welcomed the young conqueror of distant seas back to the island.

"Just look at yer old man, Noume. Ya made his hair

pretty well white with yer New Found Lands. But ya sure didn't kill yerself, did ya. Oh, but what's all this finnin and sinnin these days! A man comes home from cod and whores like he's been to a weddin, not missin a hair, nor a stump of a tooth, nor a paw, neither. It ain't Christian, this fishin ain't, lemme tell ya."

After this improvised speech, La Sagouine mopped her brow and yielded the podium to Don l'Orignal, who began to inspect his son. Noume had put on weight, god-almightyhellfire! He was the picture of health. Michel-Archange came next to inquire about his best catches and got a punch in the ribs and a burst of laughter in the face from the spirited hero.

"I caught cod, cod, and more cod. Then on top of that, a dozen beautiful tanned broads."

Right away the bums wanted to go search the hold, but Noume warned them that a good privateer never carries his treasure with him, but buries it in a safe place, watched over by the 'little grey man.' He explained immediately to La Sainte that the 'little grey man' was an ancient headless pirate who had taken it on himself to guard treasure ever since the remote ages of piracy. La Sainte retorted that they had badly needed the 'little grey man' to keep the late Sam Amateur from coming out of his tomb the evening when his damned soul had set fire to the church. But these historic comments were soon drowned in the wailings of the accordion and guitar which announced to the whole kingdom the return of the Prodigal Son.

So Noume began to tell his bold friends and faithful subjects about the adventures and misadventures of his expedition. He described distant beautiful princesses sleeping in enchanted woods who welcome you at first because they are forced to by the government and who say to you, "Yes, sah." They invite you to return because you come from far away and they have brothers in the navy, too. Then they say, "O corse, ma deah" and throw themselves at your feet and hang on to your duds and mew and complain and murmur, "Hmmm . . ." and whisper beautiful things to you.

"Sluts," said La Sagouine.

"That's a fisherman's life," answered a bum.

"Slut of a fish, too," replied the heroic woman.

"Still them sluts gave La Sagouine all her men," Noume let fly from the height of his wagon.

"Men!" bristled La Sagouine. "Gave me one and I took him, like all women who serves their country."

Then Don l'Orignal cast his royal balm over the heated dispute.

"Ya don't have to apologize so much, La Sagouine. The priest says in the Holy Scripture there's one dame who took seven men. And her name was just like yers, La Samarigouine."

Then, turning to his son, Don l'Orignal frowned with his left eyebrow. "Gotta warn ya, Noume, we's had a bit a trouble on the island these days past."

"Listen to yer old man, Noume. He'll tell ya all about it," said La Sagouine.

And immediately she made an effort to reveal to the heir apparent the unstable and ambiguous state of diplomatic relations between Flea Island and the mainland. The valorous knight Noume answered this gloomy tale by giving the noble lady a hard slap on the rump. He uttered a dreaded battle cry.

"Just let em come, the sons of bitches! Lemme at em! Ahoy! Ahoy!"

And all Flea Island understood that henceforth the tiller of the island would be in the hands of their young lord and master, Noume.

Don l'Orignal placed his spruce sceptre on his son's shoulder, solemnly saying, "Go to it, me boy, we ain't got so many that another man ain't welcome here."

Getting up off his knee, the new knight replied to his father's airs with a wry smile. Then he marched straight to the shore, followed by his faithful companions, Citrouille and Michel-Archange.

Chapter Seven

Concerning the strange apparition seen on the sea by the citizens of the mainland.

Unfortunately for him, the lighthouse keeper had abandoned his tower to the angels' watch while he paid a fleeting visit to his wine barrel. For the rest of his life the poor keeper would bewail that fatal minute which almost cost his country its peace and tranquillity. For it was precisely that very minute which the mayor, in the company of her faithful lieutenants, chose to reconnoitre by the tower. Fixing her nose to the spyglass, what a sight the brave woman beheld in the direction of Flea Island! A red glow emerged from the water as if the very depths of the sea were on fire.

"The ghost ship," cried the barber.

And all the brave civil servants and members of the mainland parliament shuddered at what these words presaged.

For a century and a half now, the inhabitants of the shores of my country have periodically glimpsed the strange phenomenon of a ship in flames drifting on the horizon with sinister slowness. It was an enormous sailing ship, rigged with masts and ropes where busy sailors climbed up and down. The entire vessel and its crew were ablaze with a fire that lit up the whole sky.

"The fire of bad weather," howled the milliner.

This ghost ship had never failed to appear the day before a great storm and it was a very foolhardy fisherman who would ignore this dark warning from the other world! For there was no doubt left in any mind as to the origin and nature of this phenomenon: the ghost ship came from hell.

The villagers told how this ominous sailboat was none other than an old vessel from the colonial period, which (according to some) had engaged in shady trade or which (according to others) had been guilty of abducting a young half-breed girl. In any case, an Indian mother skilled in witchcraft had cast a spell on the unfortunate ship. The devils had carried out the spell to the letter. That same evening, the boat burned at sea, triggering one of the most terrible storms ever seen on this side of the ocean. And ever since, the same boat was doomed to repeat its tragic journey on the eve of every storm.

Try as they might to convince themselves that this ominous fate was well deserved, that illegal trade never pays, and that all base sins are punished sooner or later, the inhabitants of the coast remained no less terrified at each vision.

And so that evening heaven bestowed its dire warning once again on the mayor and her staff. For if the devil himself should appear before that noble gathering it could only be a warning from heaven. But what did heaven want from them? That was the question.

"A ghost is still a ghost," said the barber reflectively.

"That depends," corrected the merchant.

"Depends on what?" asked the schoolmaster.

"That depends on its constitution," answered the nursing sister.

And the banker assented.

For some time they remained spellbound by the immense sea stretched out at the foot of the tower. The barber continued, "Just the same, the flaming ship is a ghost."

But the banker answered, "However, a ghost is ordinarily a man."

Then the merchant explained, "Ordinarily. But a ghost is never ordinary."

And everybody stopped talking. For the ship with all its rigging aflame had just sunk to the bottom of the sea once more.

The mayor, who had not thrown her weighty opinion into this altercation, turned the spyglass in the direction of Flea Island and saw a makeshift camp on its left bank. There was Sir Noume with his troops, bivouacking, battling and buffooning around the remains of a great fire.

Chapter Eight

Wherein is related the famous battle of Michel-Archange with a hell-hound.

While the mayor and the dignitaries of her state were watching the changing ghost ship in the night, the army of Sir Noume listened to the magnificent story of Sam Amateur around the fire. This Iliad of Flea Island was known to all who lived there, but they never grew tired of hearing it. And on festive occasions, such as the eve of battle, Pamphile, the poet laureate, would relate the epic of his island.

Once upon a time at the eastern tip of Flea Island called Pointe Enragée, there lived a formidable wild duck hunter. This hunter wielded his rifle with such fiery dexterity, that in less than twenty years he had killed off or exiled five species of sea bird: the woodcock, the crane, the seagull, the Canada goose and the black brant. Only the duck still resisted him at the time of the great event which was to change the destiny of this famous hunter of the seas and imperil the prosperity of the country.

In order to understand fully our hero's personality and to fathom the sense of the words spoken to him which put the spark to the powder, it must be made clear right away that Sam Amateur, the dangerous hunter, hunted as well on land as at sea, by night as by day, the featherless bird of the street as well as the feathered one in the sky.

One morning when Sam, lying flat on his belly in his punt, followed with his keen eye the nervous flight of a worried, distressed duck, he heard the voice of the oyster fisherman, Michel, coming from a neighbouring dory.

"Sam Amateur, ain't all the woodcocks and cranes on the island enough fer ya? Ain't ya gonna leave us a few feathers to soften our mattresses?"

Sam Amateur took the insult badly. And without

further ceremony or military protocol, he turned the barrel of his rifle in Michel's direction and fired.

On the island it has always been said that Michel was a hero predestined for great things and that his celestial namesake himself protected him that day from the invincible shot of Sam Amateur. Nobody ever knew what became of the bullet. According to fishermen who were there, it never reached the sea. Many people still believe it came so fast that it passed right through Michel's chest without leaving a mark. Others prefer to believe that it struck the invulnerable hide of the deep-water fisherman and bounced away. At any rate, none of these hypotheses has ever been proven and Michel-Archange himself has always maintained a death-like silence about this detail.

This was the first encounter of the two most valiant warriors of the sea. The fisherman Michel hunted the depths of the water just as the hunter Sam fished its surface. Between these two giants the sea trembled.

On Flea Island it was told that Sam Amateur, son of Mateur and Mathilda, devoted his nights to the witch-canoe. Winter and summer he would climb aboard a great wooden sleigh and, with the devil's help, fly away body and soul over his island towards the South Seas. La Sainte swore that he danced and frolicked all night with girls from foreign countries. But Don l'Orignal believed that the illustrious hunter's visits to the night sky were a military tactic.

Nevertheless, since that incident of the lost bullet, Sam Amateur had shown a disgraceful lack of interest in ducks. He had found in Michel-Archange an adversary more his own size. He, Sam, might be unbeatable, but Michel was unbeaten. And highborn souls do not measure valour by lost bullets.

For three months the two giants had waged total war, laying traps for each other, building barricades, waiting in ambush, calling each other names, insulting each other, grandly blowing noses at each other—all without a single hair being lost on either side. But then one fine day a trivial incident brought the knightly epic to a hasty conclusion.

Sam Amateur learned from a neighbourhood witch that his terrible adversary sometimes left the bed of Lady Sagouine to ruffle the feathers of a foreign princess by the name of La Cruche. The dreaded hunter resolved to strike while the iron was hot. He gathered a few mercenaries of his trade, handed out weapons and secretly revealed his strategy to his first lieutenant. And one dark night the army marched on the enemy entrenchments.

Michel the invulnerable, having got wind of the expedition from a rival of the first witch, set his men in ambush around the mill of his beloved princess. And it was there, at the foot of this tower, that the most awesome duel ever witnessed on Flea Island took place.

The Samists on the left and the Michelists on the right sat down in the hay to watch their leaders in fearsome and wonderful single combat. Long would the people on Flea Island talk of it, praising the strength of fist, the dexterity of foot, the vigour of biting and clawing. Everybody howled, spat, clapped, and chopped the air with their arms, swearing by all the devils of hell and Flea Island. When the dust had settled, Sam Amateur carried off the prize, La Cruche's petticoat, which he hung on a stick and planted in the prow of his punt.

For three days the Samist army celebrated this victory and its prize, La Cruche's petticoat, while Michel, entrenched in his camp, gnawed on his helmet, thinking about vengeance.

Having reached this point in his narrative, Pamphile the bard stopped to pay a short visit to his crock, the mere name of La Cruche making his mouth water.

Chapter Nine

Wherein is continued and concluded the incredible story of the invincible Sam Amateur, enemy of Michel-Archange.

After refreshing himself, the poet took up his narrative where he had left off, that is to say at La Cruche's petticoat.

He told how the intrepid Sam Amateur, since the famous conquest of the enemy flag, no longer curbed his audacity and boastfulness. He displayed the most insolent arrogance towards Michel and the Michelists and all fishermen of oysters, smelt and cod. Sam Amateur was a bold man, but he made one mistake: he underestimated the resources and the luck of the great Archangel's protégé. And this miscalculation was going to cost poor Sam a piece of skin just big enough to lead him to the grave.

Since his defeat, Michel-Archange had not left his shack. And to all those who made inquiries after his health or his plans, he invariably replied that he was on the watch for snow. Many people concluded from this that a blow from Sam must have cracked his skull, and they dismissed him as a madman. But fierce Michel just kept on waiting for winter.

Then one day in December the first snow fell. Everybody was keeping a lookout for the emergence of Archange but he didn't appear. He waited another two weeks for a second blanket of snow to cover the whole island, then he drew himself up to his full height in front of his fortifications.

It was only much later that the inhabitants of Flea Island understood the full significance of Michel-Archange's gesture. It was reported that he had built with his own hands an enormous snowman of the size and features of Sam Amateur. He was heard pronouncing some unintelligible words over the effigy, then he was seen making a hole in the monster's gut with his pitchfork. That done, he went back into his shack and waited for the mild weather to finish off his snowman. It was not long in coming. A night of wind and rain melted the snow and the next morning Sam Amateur was found dead in his bed.

The Flea Islanders have expounded at length on this mysterious affair. All sorts of hypotheses, opinions and counter-opinions were expressed without ever arriving at a satisfactory explanation. Some even dared the most irreverent speculations. A toothless and somewhat brainless old man stupidly went so far as to swear in all innocence before the court of Don l'Orignal that he had seen Michel, with his pitchfork in his right hand, prowling around Sam Amateur's shack the evening of that fatal night. Nobody dared lift the dead man's shirt, but they searched his cabin and La Cruche's petticoat was never found.

Pamphile paused here for a long time. Seeing that he was not going to begin again, his eager listeners cried out all together, "Then what? Tell us what happened then!"

Then the poet laureate closed his eyes, breathed deeply, and added to his epic the fine epilogue that follows.

The late Sam Amateur had been buried three weeks, buried alone beside the water. The Flea Islanders only talked about him in order to revive memories of his diabolical practices with the witch-canoe. One person remembered having seen him one night while he was still alive, rowing with all his might in the sky and shouting words no Christian would dare repeat. Another recalled seeing him in the morning, returning to the island covered with sweat, as if from a long and perilous journey. Sam Amateur had given or sold himself to the devil, there was no doubt about that. And he was better off dead, surely.

Better dead? The dead man might not be of the same opinion as the island on this theological issue. And he was going to make them see this.

It was the famous evening of the third week when the late Sam chose to remind the living of his memory. Everything was so quiet on the island that evening, one could imagine oneself back in the remote time of the fleas, called the Flea Age in the geological annals of the island. The first to see this event was a Flea child, as it is written that such things are revealed to little ones. He saw a wisp of fire as big as a wolf rising from the shore, right above the grave of Sam Amateur. The following evening, the apparition revealed itself to the women, then to Don l'Orignal himself. And on the third day, in the middle of a stormy night, several witnesses saw the same phenomenon come forth from the grave of the hell-hound and soar over to the church. The same night this building burned down, leaving not so much as a stone standing.

Then all eyes turned to Michel-Archange. He who had bested the living should now triumph over the dead. The devastation must be stopped, the spell must be broken. Michel-Archange understood that neither he nor the island would ever live in peace if the malicious and evil ghost were not forced to be silent. And, summoning the most tremendous courage ever granted to a single man, Flea Island's hero undertook his battle against the dead. This famous single combat of the knightly wars lasted three days and three nights and after this the conqueror returned home exhausted but happy, conscious of having saved the kingdom from the most fearful danger it had ever incurred.

What had happened between the two combatants? It is known for certain that Sam Amateur's grave was found empty after the fight. As for the rest, nothing can be sworn. Claiming to have the terrible truth from a reliable source, some said that Michel had pursued his enemy right up to the forbidden gates of hell and had even come face to face with the Evil One himself. According to the most ardent Michelists, he had glimpsed a dozen well-known faces from the mainland and a couple of Flea Islanders through a chink in the dreaded gate. The names of these honourable people, however, were never recorded in the chronicles of the island.

Thus concluded the famous epic of Flea Island, as it was sung by her poet laureate to the bivouacked troups of Sir Noume the evening when the mysterious ghost ship appeared to the people of the mainland. Pamphile, in honour of the best works by his poet colleagues of all ages, called his epic the *Fleaiade*.

Chapter Ten

Concerning the famine which raged on the island and the second expedition of Flea Islanders to capture the keg of molasses.

Don l'Orignal secretly dispatched Lady Sagouine to his son Noume with the order to report next day to the royal palace where the best minds in the kingdom were to discuss the serious events of the day. La Sagouine acquitted her mission with her usual speed and passion and brought Noume back the same evening.

"Yer father sent me fer ya," she flung at him on arriving in the camp.

Leaving his troops under Michel-Archange, Noume was accompanied by half a dozen of his bold followers: Citrouille, Boy à Polyte, Soldat-Bidoche and the bums. These parliamentarians followed La Sagouine all along the coast as she told them about the subject at issue in the debate.

All night the leaders of the country argued the question of the island's safety, threatened as it was by the most fearful famine ever recorded in the annals of the country. Some maintained that the sea was to blame since it no longer provided cod; others that the cod were to blame for devouring the herrings' eggs. Some blamed the herrings' eggs themselves. Still others blamed the dredgers for emptying the sea of its herring and cod at one and the same time. But all were agreed on one point: no matter where the trouble came from, it had to be put right.

"Christ, we can't just start layin them herrin eggs," complained La Sainte.

"Hell, I knows some as'll never lay nothin else," added Boy à Polyte.

But before fighting broke out, l'Orignal nipped it in the bud.

"Shut up, godalmightyhellfire! Neither yer shoutin nor yer eggs'll get us dinner."

There was only one solution left for the economists of Flea Island: if they have no bread, let them eat cake. The keg of molasses the merchant in town refused to sell them must be captured at any cost. And the discussion turned to molasses.

Don l'Orignal turned to the elders of the kingdom who were sitting peacefully chewing their tobacco around an earthenware spittoon. They didn't stir immediately. Then the eldest moved his dog-like ear, chewed three times on his quid and said in an even but serious voice, "Before his late death my late father grabbed a case of salt cod to feed his family that was starvin to death. God forgive him."

And all the other gray heads responded to this contribution with more energetic chewing.

Then Citrouille came and said, "That ain't the way things is. Let's go work fer our food. And if them fish a just stopped runnin, let's sign on across the way and earn them kegs of molasses."

Poor Citrouille had scarcely finished his sentence when Boy à Polyte and Soldat-Bidoche and the bums jumped on him to explain syllogistically that the mainlanders didn't sell to the islanders; that the islands could starve to death without raising an eyebrow on the mainland; that men of good will had all died in the flood; and that, if God is dead, anything is permitted. Citrouille wasn't so sure about the role of God and the flood in this matter, but he felt that in a single sentence he had exhausted the very fount of his argument, so he kept quiet.

On principle, the debate continued for several hours, but the whole assembly knew from the moment of the elders' intervention that the gauntlet had been cast and that they would march on the capital.

Noume informed Michel-Archange who assembled the troops.

Chapter Eleven

Concerning the beautiful prayers that Don l'Orignal and La Sainte offered to God for the island's well-being.

The army got under way at dawn. La Sagouine had beaten it by a good half hour. She had been entrusted by Don l'Orignal himself to reconnoitre strategic places, a mission which she carried out, as we shall see, to the great satisfaction of the Flea intelligentsia. Noume marched at the head of his troop, boiling with holy wrath and armed with poles, forks, picks, slingshots, heddles, shovels, and branches. All these bold Flea people filled the island's punts and dorys, advancing solemnly over the surging sea towards glory and molasses.

Meanwhile, Lord Don l'Orignal went off to the royal chapel to pray for the success of the expedition and the salvation of the soldiers' souls. There he found La Sainte in the process of besieging heaven in terms that left God no choice. "God the Father," she said piously, "it's ya I'm talkin to. Mind ya don't pretend ya don't hear me. Ya know Citrouille's gone off to war. Ain't nothin funny about them wars. My son just might break somethin, lemme tell ya. And it's up to you to keep an eye on him. I brought Citrouille into this here world, I sure did, but I can't keep him alive *vitam aeternatam* all by myself."

Don l'Orignal respected La Sainte's silence for a minute, and then he addressed God. "Good Lord, fer the love of Christ just listen to La Sainte prayin fer her son. Then ya gotta gimme my turn, cause I got one, too. He's a god-almightyhellfire, Noume is, I know that. But ya does what ya can with the kids ya got."

Then La Sainte began again. "What I'm asking ya, God the Father Almighty, is to bring back my Citrouille as lively as I gave him to ya twenty years ago. And I promise ya I'll wear my medals all the blessed days of me life till the end of me days, and death do us part. I'll do thirty-three stations of the cross, too, one right after the other, if that's yer holy will and command."

Don l'Orignal continued in turn, "It ain't just Noume I'm askin ya to bring back, Good Lord. If ya wants to save the others too it'd fix things real good down here. There ain't very many of us on the island. Every man counts, and each one's got his woman and ship's boys in his house. And ya know yerself: no war, no molasses; no molasses, no life. Amen."

"Good Lord, save me boy fer the love of the blessed sons of Zebediah," shouted La Sainte.

"Spare the men over there and deliver the island from hunger," prayed Don l'Orignal.

"Spare the world from the tricks and fancy ways of the devil," continued the saintly woman.

"Deliver us from famine, war, and all pestilence," added the king.

"Bless us above all women by yer son Jesus, fruit of our wombs," beseeched the weeping mother.

"And spare all men of good will," sighed the poor man, letting his full snow-white beard flow down over his breast.

And silence once more flooded the little pine chapel, blending with the perfume of ferns and dandelions. Then, although the sky was clear that night and seemed incapable of sudden change, La Sainte added the prayer for bad weather to ward off all contingencies and leave no opening for fate.

"Lord deliver us from thunder, lightnin, foul winds, foul rain, foul harrycane. If the thunder strikes, make it strike where it won't do no harm. If it strikes, make it strike as stone, so be it. Amen."

When Don l'Orignal left the temple, he saw all the noisy little brats of the country swarming in the hay, shouting out to announce La Sagouine's return. The king's spy confidently made her way towards the palace and sat under the colonnade to catch her breath. The women and children of the kingdom at once grouped around the royal emissary and waited, open-mouthed, for a declaration about the country's fate. Gradually, La Sagouine was able to collect enough breath in her throat and enough impressions in her head to begin her tale of the battle and give an account of her mission to her lord and master, Don l'Orignal.

Chapter Twelve

Wherein are told the glorious exploits of Sir Noume.

La Sagouine told how, stepping onto the mainland, she first unloaded her belongings, then made her way with her bucket, mop and dust rags to the barber shop. Unnoticed, she was able to get the gist of the conference between the barber and the schoolmaster.

"I come to shine yer place up," she said to the master of the store.

And when the storekeeper was about to object, she cut him off short.

"It's yer wife sent me, barber."

No barber in the world could have countered this argument. So the barber of the town in question said nothing.

In order to camouflage her intentions better and make them forget her presence, La Sagouine tried hard to blend into the walls, the floor, her bucket and dust rags, thus drowning her individuality and her mission in the great universal charbucket of the world. She modelled all her movements on the barber's: daubing the floor as the barber soaped a chin; scraping with the mop as he skinned with the razor; rubbing with the dust rag as he sponged with the towel.

Through this cunning strategy she had been able to pick up all the most consequential pieces of news as they came tumbling into her bucket. Thus she had learned that the new catechisms would not arrive for the beginning of school; that the assistant librarian was suffering from a mysterious stomach ailment and ate only a small potato for dinner; that each day young people appeared more depraved and more disrespectful; that a certain teacher taught audacious things in socio-mathematical botany; and that very soon, the whole world would see what it costs a country to feed ungodly persons who no longer want to rest on Sundays.

The liaison agent of the F.S.S. (Flea Secret Service) revealed all this precious information to the Flea Islanders crowded around Don l'Orignal's stump.

While in their native land people were pondering the latest news from the front, over across the sea Flea Island's army was immortalizing its unknown soldiers. The landing had taken place in the west in order to foul up the enemy's calculations, since it was one of the most established military theories of the mainlanders that the devil always came from the east. Then General Noume had sent a first detachment in the direction of the drygoods and millinery store to prevent the milliner from appearing at the merchant's, while three other squadrons looked after the bank, the school and the hospital. As for the barber shop, it was left to La Sagouine, whose artillery of buckets and mops was equal to the weapons of an entire regiment.

The town was so surprised to find itself suddenly invaded by foreigners moving about on the square, in the streets and around the principal public buildings, that nobody dared move from his window or cash register that day. Every respectable man shut himself in with a padlock, sat on his riches, and didn't stir.

When Noume sensed that life on the mainland had stopped, that all the foxes were in their dens and the hares in their burrows, he judged that the hour had come. So he sent General Michel-Archange with the left wing to the right and Citrouille at the head of the right wing to the left. Noume kept the centre for himself. The target for all three armies was the keg of molasses.

The regiment of Michelists was the first to reach the enemy zone. It was a batallion of bold and courageous men who had already won renown in several expeditions of this nature, especially during the Samic Wars. The army corps commanded by Noume arrived on the spot at almost the same time. It had been delayed by a troop of altar boys on their annual picnic who were sitting in the daisies, innocently barring the road against the marching army.

"Where's Citrouille?" inquired Noume on joining Michel-Archange.

"The devil only knows."

The devil knew only too well.

Skirting the merchant's vegetable garden, Citrouille suddenly stopped as if taken by a fit of trembling or dizziness. Through a gap in the picket fence he had just caught sight of the vision which had haunted all his nights since the fatal day he first saw his chosen princess bathing on the shores of the mainland. There she was this day, sitting stiffly on the swing and singing. Forgetting everything—Noume, the war, the molasses—Citrouille the lover jumped over the fence.

Noume began to grow impatient.

"Where the devil godalmighty bejeezus tarnation is Citrouille?"

Citrouille was already far away.

While Noume and Michel-Archange's troops swore and spat, hidden behind the warehouse of the general store, happy Citrouille was spouting the most beautiful sentences of his whole life at the foot of the swing. He would fish for oysters winter and summer, under ice or sun; he would make a fortune; he would build a house, a pretty little house with a fireplace and shutters; he would go to church every Sunday with a hat and a yellow tie and shoes that squeaked and a bouquet for the lady of his heart. The lady of his heart listened to her lover's delirium without flinching or turning a hair. Straight, pale and pure. Citrouille caught his breath and continued with renewed vigour. He would go far away if necessary, he would cross oceans, he would slay beasts, he would kill giants, he would lay siege to cities, provinces, continents, he would conquer the world and lay it at the feet of his beloved.

Had the merchant caught wind of the assault on his daughter, or had he merely noticed Citrouille's men milling about in his garden? Nobody could say. But what everybody could see with his own eyes was that the storekeeper hurried away from his store and headed for the backyard of his house with an eloquent step.

With this unhoped-for retreat of the enemy, Noume and

Michel-Archange saw luck smiling on them and wasted no time. They didn't wait for Citrouille's reinforcements, but charged immediately in the direction of the keg which they seized in less time than it took Citrouille to cross back over the boundary from forbidden territory.

The capture of the keg and Citrouille's rout with the right wing happened so rapidly and in so much confusion that it is impossible for an author who wishes to be faithful to the strictest truth to begin to tell the tale. But one true fact is beyond doubt and deserves to be reported: the merchant's defeat. For finding himself caught between his daughter and his keg of molasses, he had wanted (like a true business man) to negotiate with the other side. And thus he had seen Citrouille escape him while he ran after his molasses, and then, correcting his aim and dashing off on the trail of Citrouille, he had seen his keg roll to the shore.

When Flea Island's army returned from this first skirmish, only one man was missing.

Chapter Thirteen

Concerning the search made throughout the kingdom for Citrouille.

After jamming his horned crown down over his forehead, Don l'Orignal, surrounded by old men, women and children, made his way towards the shore. The king and his subjects had been waiting there for several hours when the harsh sound of the accordion struck their ears and stirred their hearts. At once an enormous cheer rose from Flea Island, torn simultaneously from all throats, from throughout the hay, from all the sands by the waiting sea, "Here they come!"

Indeed the dauntless soldiers of Noume and Michel-Archange were coming. Standing in their dorys, caps over their ears, wearing daisies for boutonnières, they sensually stroked the big round belly of the keg of molasses that rolled about at the mercy of the waves. It was Flea Island's finest hour.

Noume and Michel-Archange were carried in triumph to Victory Square in the centre of the island. And a monument was erected there to commemorate the defeat of the merchant and all the citizens of the mainland. Three wheelbarrows turned upside down, their shafts forming a six-pointed star, served as a base for the illustrious keg. It was more beautiful than all the triumphal arches, the eternal flames and the unknown soldiers of all the war memorials in the world. For this keg was more than a monument, more than a symbol of victory—it was the fountain of youth, the Flea Islanders' tree of life.

This was more or less the gist of the speech given by the poet laureate, Pamphile, during the inauguration of the keg. He was about to tackle the peroration addressed to the valiant soldiers when his lines were drowned out by the dramatic prose of La Sainte who had just noticed Citrouille's absence.

Citrouille didn't answer the roll call. Citrouille hadn't returned. Where was Citrouille? Don l'Orignal wanted to quiet La Sainte, but the crowd was already alarmed, electrified. A man was missing.

This time Don l'Orignal himself took command of the volunteers. He organized a beating to force the game out of the woods. The women divided the chief compass points of the island among themselves and the men jumped into their boats to search the sea. In less than five minutes there wasn't a cat left in Victory Square where only the abandoned keg remained enthroned.

While the population was beating hay, dunes, seaweed and the water's depths on the island and at sea, La Sagouine, without saying a word, had straddled her birch-bark canoe and was paddling towards the mainland at breakneck speed. La Sagouine was used to diplomatic missions. More than once she had received the island's plenipotentiary powers. And when they weren't granted to her, she knew how to take them.

Once more Flea Island's spy had seen clearly. Landing on terra firma, she made straight for the picket fence which surrounded the merchant's property. And there, crawling on her belly in the couch grass, she discovered Citrouille, camouflaged under the wild rhubarb, sending desperate signals in the direction of a window with closed shutters.

When towards sunset La Sagouine handed the despondent Citrouille back to his mother, there wasn't a shred of hay left standing or a reed half-broken on Flea Island. The Samic Wars had not ravaged the island more than this royal hunt throughout the kingdom in search of La Sainte's son.

But while the keg of molasses was being emptied to celebrate his return, La Sainte's son ate his heart out, vowing that the sun would never shine for him again.

Chapter Fourteen

Concerning the great conference that took place on the mainland and the strange illness from which the merchant's daughter Adeline suffered.

The same evening as the Flea Islanders' victory over the keg, the mayor lectured the assembled citizens of the town.

Gradually feelings became heated. It was the schoolmaster who first shouted, "Down with Don l'Orignal!" And the whole crowd echoed, "Down with Flea Island!" Seeing this nation of noble and honourable people baring their teeth and claws that day, any witness would have concluded that it was all over for the enemy kingdom; that the courageous and innocent little island tossing happily on the sea had only a few more hours of life and that Flea Island was going to perish under the force of the war-like fury kindled by the indomitable mayor.

However, the gods had decided otherwise. The hour of Flea Island had not yet come. And that evening it was the merchant in spite of himself who saved the island.

When the merchant had despaired of getting his keg back, he had tried his best to save the most he could from the massacre and, for want of anything better, had fallen back on his daughter. Now he found her shut up in her room, listless and suffering from a strange fever. Under this second blow, the merchant panicked and came running to the square where the whole town was holding counsel.

"Adeline is sick! Adeline is dying!" he yelled in front of the already deeply disturbed people.

The crowd of solid citizens lost no time. It felt a great need that day to march on something. And, unable to march on the water to reach Flea Island, it made a pilgrimmage instead to the window of Adeline, innocent victim of the barbarians' attack.

The innocent victim spent the night in a complete daze while her mysterious illness spread through all her limbs. At daybreak it came to lodge in the region of her heart and loins. In the morning the doctor gave his prognosis: the merchant's daughter would not get well.

Chapter Fifteen

Concerning the many fruitless efforts of the townsfolk to bring the fair Adeline back to health.

The merchant's daughter did not get well. However, her illness wrought no other havoc than to make her insensible to everything that used to interest and amuse her. She didn't laugh, play or sing any more, scarcely ate and hardly slept at all. She spent every morning on her balcony and the afternoons in the swing, dreaming of some unexpected event that would deliver her from her sickness and her prison. Yet when Adeline was asked what she was suffering from, her gaze fluttered over the sea and she murmured, "I don't know."

Despairing of saving his daughter, the merchant nevertheless listened to the townsfolk who bombarded him with advice ranging from chiropractics to palmistry after exhausting the whole range of psychology, psychiatry, psychoanalysis, psychotechnics and psychotherapy. The worthy merchant, not knowing which way to turn among all these sciences, leaned instead in the direction of the banker who suggested a trip to tropical climates. But Adeline would hear none of it and clung with all her might to her swing and her balcony.

Then the mayor and the milliner had the idea of sending the country's most dashing youths to the invalid in the hope of bringing her out of her lethargy. The sons of the wealthy townsfolk came to strut in front of the picket fence, performing all sorts of gymnastics and acrobatics: agonistics, spheristics, jumping, running, boxing, fencing, high-jumping, hoop-rolling, trapeze-swinging, wrestling and judo. But the mere sight of their white hands and powdered moustaches sickened the poor girl, who had not forgotten the exotic fragrance of sea and salt grasses. So the sons of the barbers, the bankers and the schoolmasters were obliged to go away again, crestfallen.

One morning before dawn, Adeline left her balcony, passed by her swing without stopping and walked straight to the dock. And there, with her bare feet skimming the foam, she watched the sun come out of the sea and light up the tin chimneys one by one, as Flea Island was snatched from the night. She remained facing the water like this for hours, alone with a dream too big for her tiny size, searching the sea for a ripple which might have been caused by a pebble tossed in another world.

Meanwhile, the other world trembled with the same emotion. Every leaf of clover quivered in tune with the heart of the poor young man dreaming on a dune of white sand. Since the skirmish of his people on the mainland, Citrouille wanted nothing of molasses or fishing. Nothing, nobody. He spent his days at the extreme tip of the island with his feet dug into the soft sand, always whistling the same little tune he had heard one day in a swing.

La Sainte and Don l'Orignal had tried everything to snap Citrouille out of it: prayers, threats, promises, revels, traps, tricks, jokes and, as a last resort, La Cruche. But none of it could free the young man from his melancholy. He continued to drag his poor heart in a sling over the sands of his dune.

Now this morning of Adeline's first visit to the dock, Citrouille felt a new emotion prickling under his skin. His sadness seemed to melt quickly before some strange and marvellous force, something very close to courage and daring. That same morning, Citrouille had a great dream and began to concoct his incredible plan.

Chapter Sixteen

Concerning the ingenious strategy of the lover Citrouille and the gracious counterstroke of the mayor.

For three days Citrouille peeled the white tender bark (called 'mashkoui' in his country) from the few birches on Flea Island. On their backs he carved hearts pierced by arrows and topped with gothic initials. Then, gathering all these tender messages, he crammed them into bottles, jugs, even a little barrel decked with a mast and sail. Citrouille was not one to divide his eggs between two baskets. He launched his entire fleet all at once on the sea.

The channel separating Flea Island from the mainland had never seen anything like it. One fine morning it woke up to the tickling and swishing of a multitude of little boats invading its waters, like the navy of Lilliput attacking the empire of Blefuscu. The bottles and jugs floated peacefully, blown by the current and the morning breeze, rolling their rounded bellies where Citrouille's great secret was kept warm.

On the opposite shore the same morning, the town children were building fantastic sand castles. They frequently ran to the sea to fill their big conch shells with salt water to make them solid. And so it was that one of them first caught sight of the Lilliputian fleet. When the castle builder sounded the alarm, all the brave little ships' boys on their knees in the sand lifted their heads, jumped up and climbed the steep cliff as fast as their legs would carry them. And there, squeezed against each other in the most holy silence, they beheld the enemy fleet heading straight towards them.

Suddenly one of them shouted, "They're bottles!"

Immediately the most confident climbed down the cliffs on all fours, followed by any others willing to leave their fate to God.

Before the town hall clock chimed noon, the whole village knew about the mysterious affair of the miniature fleet from the south. It could only be a provocation or a declaration of war. And without losing any time, the schoolmaster and the milliner began to decipher the code.

"A for Alphonse," said the milliner. "That isn't very difficult. That code's been used to death in wars."

"But C?" asked the teacher. "Do they mean cavalry? Camp? Cannon? Campaign or counterattack?"

"C seems to me to have a rather shady scatological meaning," replied the milliner, pinching her nose.

"Maybe they're alluding to the Christian era," risked the schoolmaster.

"The Christian era, my dear master, is symbolized by A.D. Why then C?"

"To divert suspicion," said the learned man maliciously. He had read Machiavelli's *Prince* three times.

Meanwhile, the mayor had approached the merchant, inquiring about the identity of the young lover who had prowled around his daughter on the fatal day of the Flea attack. But the merchant had had too many other fish to fry that day to take note of appearances or remember names. At the most, and very vaguely at that, he remembered having heard someone call his friend by the strange name of a fruit or vegetable.

"C," murmured the mayor. "C for cucumber? For carrot? For cabbage?"

The mayor cast her eye about her, then whispered in the merchant's ear, "Put your daughter in a nunnery, merchant. We must leave nothing to chance this time. Leave the rest to me."

The rest was a well thought-out plan to reconquer the stolen keg and settle accounts with Flea Island. The mayor had been swearing to put her enemies in their place for such a long time that she wasn't sorry to have found the opportunity. And a keg of molasses was a small price to pay for the destruction of a little island which had gotten too big for its britches and was beginning to get in her way.

"Shut your daughter up in a nunnery," the noble woman repeated, squinting in the direction of the island she had sworn to destroy. "And now it's between the two of us!"

The merchant, thinking she meant him, smiled back at his sovereign. But the mayor was grinning to herself, while gazing beyond the merchant's head at her bitterest enemy.

Chapter Seventeen

Wherein is narrated the most elegant chassé-croisé ever danced on the high sea.

The mayor, who had sent the lighthouse keeper to find out about Adeline's secret suitor, was rewarded beyond all hope. She learned that Don l'Orignal, wishing to divert the young lover from his strange listlessness—the young lover who was called Citrouille and not Cabbage or Carrot—was organizing a hunting party here on the mainland.

The mayor started. "Here?"

Then, on second thought, she repeated slyly, "Here . . . you say?"

That very evening, the whole town was summoned to the square where the mayor revealed what she could of her intentions. They would take advantage of the absence of the general staff of the Flea Islanders to recapture the stolen keg. All men of an age to bear arms must report to the town hall the next day. Then, taking aside the barber, the banker, the milliner and the merchant, she let them in on the crafty schemes which this book does not dare spell out, but whose very surprising and unexpected consequences it will relate.

The keeper's information was reliable. Don l'Orignal in fact landed on the mainland in the wee hours of the morning in the joyous company of his entire court. Since the sea no longer gave cod, they had come to ask the forest for its hares and partridge. The mayor waited until the royal court of Flea Island had scattered in the woods surrounding the town. Then she gave the signal to attack. Immediately the yachts, sailboats and pleasure craft of the wealthy townsfolk filled up with the most prominent citizens and the elegant fleet steered for Flea Island.

What happened in my country that day, on the mainland and on the island, merits the praise of a new epic worthy of the pen of Flea Island's great epic poet, Pamphile. But, like roses, poets fade away and Pamphile, like most of the heroes of this drama, is no longer.

All day the sun shone with all its might, the only witness to the double hunt going on below. And as it began its decline to the west, it saw Don l'Orignal gaily blowing his horn to call his people back to the shore. The entire court rushed down the cliff, shouting and yelling loudly, and boarded ship for the island.

The keeper spied on the manoeuvres of the boats from the top of his lighthouse without stirring, and when he was sure that they were headed towards the western tip of the island, he gave the agreed signal. It was the barber who picked it up. And immediately the mayor and the townsfolk left the island, sailing along the eastern tip.

Afterwards, the lighthouse keeper was unjustly blamed for the unfortunate adventure which followed, for he was quite right in signalling the departure of the Flea Islanders towards the west. However, the unlucky keeper was nevertheless partly responsible in his short-sightedness, because a keeper who has spied on Flea Island for a good part of his life ought to have foreseen that a nation like the Flea people would never go home in a straight line. The sea is too vast and life too long for a lover of both to hurry over either on his travels. And thus the dorys and the barges of Don l'Orignal zigzagged home from the hunt, going around every buoy, every strand of seaweed, every tremor of the water lit by the evening sun.

And that was how the two fleets happened to cross.

In the Flea Islanders' camp the first to spot the enemy was La Cruche, who knew most of the solid townsfolk by their first names. She immediately warned Don l'Orignal, who drew himself up to his full height in the prow and appeared thus, crown on his head, before the enemy fleet. With a gesture the mayor ordered that the keg be hidden under oilskins and the boats speeded up. But the move had not escaped La Sagouine who recognized the shape of the keg under the cloth. Immediately she climbed to the top of the mainmast and there, with her feet wound in the rigging, she screeched so as to be heard over three oceans, "Goddam robbers!"

And the race began. The cod dorys hit the waves with all

their weight in pursuit of the elegant little white and red boats flying under full sail. Nobody will ever know which side would have carried the day, for at that moment the wind veered. Or rather all heads on the townsfolk's side turned to follow that of the merchant who had just caught sight of a birch-bark canoe far off, rocking the two illustrious lovers of our story.

"My daughter!" cried the poor weeping father. "My daughter's been kidnapped."

In the midst of all the townsfolk who lost their heads, only the mayor kept cool. She ordered them to turn about and they shot forward towards the innocent little canoe.

The sudden manoeuvre surprised and upset Don l'Orignal and his sailors. But quickly La Sagouine cried from the rigging that the enemy was chasing a canoe to the west that seemed to be carrying Citrouille. And the entire Flea Island fleet charged to the west to help Citrouille.

In the evening when the battle was over, Flea Island had lost its keg but saved its fleet, its men and its honour. In the town across the way, Adeline was taken back to her nunnery and the milliner to her house. The poor milliner, wanting to defend the trophy, had dropped, buttocks first, into the molasses.

Chapter Eighteen

Concerning the cruel anguish that tortured Citrouille.

Citrouille was fishing alone on the northern sea. Distant guitar music punctuated the slow movement of the rake scraping the bottom. With the music, a raft approached Citrouille's punt. The bums were taking Sir Noume for a ride on the vast sea that washed the shores of Flea Island.

"Ahoy! Citrouille!" shouted Noume to his loyal friend.

And, jumping from his raft, he swam towards the punt.

"Oh, fishin, me boys," sang the hero of Flea Island to the tune of 'On our way rejoicing.' "With lotsa them oysters, ya'll rake in lotsa money. And any pighead who'd rifle yer little house and its big fireplace'd better watch out!"

"A man ain't a man without a home and a fireplace," said Citrouille without raising his eyes from the sea. "He's just a guy from the island."

"Eh! A man's a man," Noume began, "on land and sea. I learned that in the old country. They tried to make trouble fer us there, too. Not everyone in the world belongs there, if you listen to them. Some folks walks this way, and some folks walks that. But one fine evenin bombs starts poppin round our heads, and that evenin, Citrouille, everybody run the same way. There wasn't nothin left on earth but men all scared shitless, on land the same as on water."

"I sure as hell ain't scared of bombs."

"Yer scared of bombs in petticoats. But they's no more dangerous, lemme tell ya. A pretty chick's like a bomb. She makes all men run the same way. On earth as in heaven."

"But it's them guys from the mainland that catches em."

"Ya just gotta run faster. Listen, Citrouille. It's the storekeeper's daughter that's got ya on the rack, eh? A nice piece of loot. But come off it, she ain't nothin but a girl. And ya got a lot to offer."

Citrouille gazed an instant at the little bluebottles

playing on the surface of the water. Then, raising his head, he said, "I ain't got nothin."

Then Noume let his feet swing aboard the punt and, gathering into a sheaf all his knowledge of man and his philosophy of nature, he explained to Citrouille, "Over in the old country I had my coat and my souwester. Nothin but that, Citrouille, and a head crammed with pretty stories. All the time we's watched them people over there livin, we's imagined their smart world hidden behind glass. Ya passes at night under their windows and before all them yellow lights, Jeezus, ya starts dreamin. Ya sees plush sofas and little tables on wheels and funny lamps and a log burnin in the fireplace and a woman in a white dress with her shoulders swayin over a piano. That's heaven, it is. But Citrouille, that's only heaven fer us poor guys from the island. Cause paradise, ya know, is either up there with the stars or right there in yer thick head."

Noume stopped talking an instant, then gave a hard kick at the sea, adding, "The day I went into their world deep in them parks, pfft . . . bust their paradise! Ya gotta look at heaven through a pane of yellow light."

"I wanna get to the other side," Citrouille declared stubbornly.

"Call her over to this here side."

"I'll cross to the other side or bust their Jeezus windows."

Noume put his big fisherman's hand on his friend's shoulder. "Ya'll bust yer nose on it and we'll have to bury ya, Citrouille."

Then, whistling for the bums, Don l'Orignal's son jumped onto the raft and drifted off to the sad music of the accordion.

Citrouille watched the youth of the island moving away and repeated softly, "We'll have to bury Citrouille . . ."

Far off, he heard an echo coming from the raft and the accordion. "We'll have to bury Citrouille."

The sad lover of Flea Island pulled his rake out of the sea and put it across the punt. Then, staring at a stray piece of seaweed that was twisting about like a sea serpent, the Flea prince said, " 'To croak or not to croak, that's the big deal.

'Is it better fer a guy from the island to drag out his bitch of a life goin between his shack and his punt, or to finish it all off by sinkin between them?

'To croak, to end it all, once and fer all.

'One Citrouille less in the world.

'To croak, to sink, to sleep, perhaps to dream.

'Yeah . . . dreams. Dream his whole life away at the bottom of the sea.

'What would a man find there?

'Oysters? And after? Nobody knows.

'That's why he hangs on to his punt.

'Cause nobody knows what he'd find at the bottom of the sea.

'Otherwise, why'd a man from the islands let himself be burgled, then punched in the mug, called names, then have his girl whistled at—all this by the people of the mainland?

'The water's cold and he's chicken, so the man hangs on to his punt.' "

And the punt carried Citrouille aimlessly adrift on the arm of the sea that cuts across my country.

Chapter Nineteen

Concerning the extraordinary discovery made at l'Anse-aux-Cochons.

The day after the mayor's expedition to the island, Boy à Polyte and Soldat-Bidoche came to find La Sagouine and invite her to follow them in top secrecy. The worthy Sagouine was not a woman to buy a secret too dearly and she bounded after them. They went around several shacks and crossed the swamp. Arriving at l'Anse-aux-Cochons, Boy à Polyte stopped and drew La Sagouine near.

"Good God! Jeezus Christ!" she cried out, seeing in the soft earth the undeniably visible print of the mayor's heel.

The mayor had come this far then. The expedition had crossed the island and that was an infraction of the laws of war! What could anybody want at l'Anse-aux-Cochons? The designs of the townsfolk surely went beyond the keg of molasses. Can't trust them bejeezus college kids. And drawing herself to her full height, La Sagouine spit into the dint left by the formidable heel.

La Sagouine bound her men to the most complete silence and crossed the swamp at marathon speed to carry the news to her lord, Don l'Orignal. By the time La Sagouine reached the royal palace, the whole island was following her, shouting that the mayor's shoe had been found at l'Anse-aux-Cochons.

In less than an hour the following items were brought from the four corners of the island to the foot of the king's stump: the banker's pipe, the teacher's pince-nez, one of the merchant's gloves, the barber's cane, a silk handkerchief and a pink garter which could only belong to the milliner.

So Don l'Orignal took counsel. The mayor and her people had searched the entire island. What could this unmentionable, immeasurable, sluttish insolence mean? And what measures should be adopted to head off the impending danger?

Meanwhile, La Sagouine turned the delicate little silk handkerchief over and over again between her gnarled fingers.

"The milliner must a been holdin her nose," she said. "When she seen her hankerchief on our rough ground all stinkin of grease and shit she didn't wanna lower herself to pick it up. Well, does she think them's gold and pearls she's gonna bury in this here hanky? Am I less snotty just cause I got a silk hanky? The corn and beans we eats grew in the shit, the milliner's same as other people's. And if the land ain't manured, couch grass and briars grow. They hold their Jeezus noses on our island! But why do they wanna take it away from us so bad?"

"It's to rub and polish it and make it all shine like a baby's bum," answered Noume.

"I'd watch out fer a baby's bum that shines too long," continued La Sagouine, screwing up an eye. "I'd make the baby eat yarrow to regulate its guts."

That said, La Sagouine made a ball with the silk handkerchief and flung it in the direction of the mainland. But La Sainte didn't let such a precious relic be lost so easily. She gathered every piece of evidence into her bag and proposed to her sovereign, Don l'Orignal, that they be kept in a museum. So on the day after the foray of the townsfolk into enemy territory, La Sainte was appointed by the Ministry of Culture to the position of first director of Flea Island's war museum.

At the precise moment when the Flea Island government was setting the holy woman up in her new office, Michel-Archange, the king's squire, pricked up his ears in the direction of the northern sea. From far away came an unusual noise: the purrrr of the townsfolk's motors which sounded so different from the put-put-put of the island's boats. Somebody was coming.

The bums' music froze. La Sagouine wanted to run and see, and Noume pushed all his men into the tall grass to begin crawling towards the shore. But Don l'Orignal brought his island to a standstill with a wave of his sceptre. This time the enemy was coming neither as an invader nor as a spy. The little boat sped along without noise or fanfare, all its sails lowered and its flag at half-mast.

Chapter Twenty

*Wherein is related the funeral eulogy
a little island gave to the mortal
remains of its so loyal, lovable and
regretted hero.*

La Sainte was the first to understand.

"Citrouille! Citrouille! They's drownded him on me!"

"Holy Mother of Jeezus Christ the Good Lord!" burst out La Sagouine. And the whole island leaned towards the little boat coming up alongside it.

The schoolmaster and the nursing sister unloaded poor Citrouille all swollen with salt water and set him down on the soft sand of his island.

Don l'Orignal stepped forward, solemn and stiff.

"Who did that?"

"He did, Don l'Orignal," answered the schoolmaster, making an effort to see through his foggy glasses. "He did it all by himself."

The Lady Sagouine threw the kerchief that kept her black mane neat at the feet of the foreigners and bawled out in a voice that could be heard over the sea, the mainland and the entire world, "All by himself? Do ya really believe things like that's done all by yerself? No, Holy Virgin Mary! Not that! A guy twenty throws himself into the sea and he does it cause he ain't got a damned bit of land to sink his feet in, fer Christ's sake. And them folks that refused him land is the ones that pushed him to the dock."

"And them folks that made fun of him," Noume added in an effort to outdo her, "is the ones that gave him a kick in the ass."

"And them folks that took his girl away is the ones that threw him into the water," finished Michel-Archange.

And the entire population of Flea Island stood silent in

respect for the noble despair of La Sainte who cried while hugging her son's sodden feet.

Then Don l'Orignal took off his four-horned crown and approached the innocent victim.

"Don't make a big deal about it, Citrouille. We's on yer side. And we's still strong, godalmightyhellfire! Ya liked them girls from the grand world too much, but ya was a good guy who knew how to rake oysters and nab cod like no other sonuvabitch. Too bad ya didn't know how to go on hopin some more, cause I'd a got yer shack fer ya to put yer wife in. But don't let it bother ya, Citrouille, the rest of us is still livin and we'll get ya yer piece a land."

"Yeah, some land to bury Citrouille!" shouted the fearless knight Noume.

And the whole crowd repeated angrily, "A piece a land to bury Citrouille!"

Then everyone picked up a shovel, a fork or a harpoon and followed their lord and master Don l'Orignal who had shoved his crown down over his eyes.

The schoolmaster and the nursing sister just had time to take a step back to let the people pass on their way to the promised land. So the whole nation was swallowed up by dorys, punts, dugouts, barges, fishing smacks, canoes, rafts, logs and anything that floats or sails on water. When the two rescuers from the mainland finally lifted their heads, they saw not a single man left on the island, but on the sea they saw a breaking wave of barbaric hordes such as the world had not seen since the Huns descended on Italy.

The schoolmaster thought for a moment about taking a short cut to warn the big town that was going quietly about its business, unaware of the sea-quake that would soon crack the foundations of its ancient civilization. But the nursing sister wasn't as far-sighted and proposed that they look after the corpse first. After all, the poor Flea man had a soul too and a body that was really too swollen and salty at the moment.

So the schoolmaster and the nursing sister made an effort to embalm Citrouille, not suspecting the surprises that the hero of romance had in store for them.

Chapter Twenty One

Concerning the tremendous gang of Flea Islanders on the mainland to avenge the memory of a courageous man.

On the mainland that morning, each townsman was busy with his little concerns, unaware what his neighbour was doing, discretion being the virtue most admired by that elite. So the banker set down rounded, well-shaped numbers in a row; the barber sharpened the teeth of his dangerous razor; the merchant caressed his cold merchandise in tin boxes; the milliner beat dust from the velvets and silks of her straw hats; and the mayor, straight-backed on her presidential throne, soberly reflected on the future of the world and her village.

This future had been insured with all the health insurance, accident insurance, fire insurance, theft insurance, life insurance and eternity insurance companies. Nothing could trouble the peace and quiet of this steadfast land, held firm by centuries of sound manners, honourable traditions, solid virtues—an old, refined and highly moral civilization. The mayor could keep her smooth brow and calm eye. The world was going well and in this world, in the little white spot which formed the village she ruled in the name of the gods, things were going even better.

"Ahoy . . . oy . . . oy! Ahoy . . . oy . . . oy!"

The mayor straightened up on her formidable heels. Her brow wrinkled and her eyes flamed. She walked to the window and there caught her breath.

"Ahoy . . . oy . . . oy!"

The barbarians had come. Every man, woman and child of them. There at the foot of the lighthouse, slicing the air

65

with their picks and shovels, howling their dreadful war cries.

The mayor let drop the curtain of her window to call the guard, but already the barber, the milliner, the banker, the merchant and all the finer people of the town had invaded the town hall.

"There they are."

"They're here."

"The Flea people."

The whole village, so peaceful scarcely an hour before, was now in complete confusion, upside down, pell mell, head first in an anarchic state without head or tail. They were afraid of being beaten, burned, eaten naked. The barber shouted and gestured, the merchant shook in his britches and the milliner called for help.

In all this general confusion, only the mayor kept her blood warm. Indeed, she felt her veins swelling with the invigorating warmth of sweet anger. And pushing aside the dense mass of terrified people in front of her, she went down the steps of the great marble staircase in the town hall one at a time. And so, alone, with her head held high, her townspeople hiding behind her, the noble lady met Don l'Orignal at the head of his people.

It was here that the first dialogue between the two tribes took place.

"What do you want?"

"Hou - hououou!"

"What does that mean?"

"Grrrr!"

"You're on our land here!"

"Chirp - chirp - chirp!"

"Go away!"

"Citrouille's dead!"

"We didn't kill him!"

"Ya sure did!"

"Get off our land."

"He drownded here."

"He wanted to seduce our girls."

"Yer girls is bitches."

"Oh!"

"And ya searched our island."

"You stole our molasses."

"We's starvin to death."

"You should have bought it."

"Ya shoulda sold it to us."

"We don't sell on credit here, and we don't trade for cod."

"Cod's made by the Good Lord just like yer trout."

"Get off our land at once."

"First we wants some land to bury Citrouille who died here."

Then, turning to his people, Don l'Orignal said, "Maybe there's lots of laws fer the livin but there's only one fer the dead: the dead owns the underworld while they's waitin to get on with the resurrection."

"Let's go, guys," shouted Noume.

"Ahoy . . . oy . . . oy! Ahoy . . . oy . . . oy!"

And the Flea nation began to move.

The mayor alone could do nothing against the commotion of an entire island, so she drew back.

Behind the nunnery under Adeline's window, Boy à Polyte and Soldat-Bidoche dug the widest and deepest grave ever intended for a living person.

Chapter Twenty Two

Concerning the mysterious blending of science and nature, whence came a great miracle.

While Citrouille's grave was being dug on the mainland, on the island the schoolmaster and the nursing sister were paying their last respects to the mortal remains.

The courageous teacher began by taking off the dead man's shirt and wet pants while the nursing sister busied herself around the shacks looking for clean clothes in La Sainte's cupboards. Then they divided the task of washing the body, the sister choosing the face and neck for her share, leaving the rest to the schoolmaster.

The two undertakers were working with all their body and soul to restore a life-like appearance to the swollen drowned man when the learned schoolmaster felt the embryo of an idea coiling around his temples. Suddenly he stared at the noble nursing sister as closely as the thickness of his glasses allowed. She almost misinterpreted the cause of this sudden ardour spreading over her partner's face.

"Eureka!" he bellowed, leaping onto his hind paws like a roused hare.

The sister, who did not understand Greek, had already seized her three-stranded rosary with one hand and with the other grabbed the end of a twisted, knotty branch.

"Eureka!" repeated the learned man, clapping his hands. "We'll embalm him."

The nursing sister drew a breath. Then, thinking better of it, "Embalm him? How? Are you the director of a funeral parlour?"

No, he wasn't a specialist in funerals but in natural science. He adored plants, whose rare nutritive, digestive, laxative, astringent and moderating virtues he recognized. The nursing sister thought she detected a whiff of heresy behind the learned man's science and strictly refused to take part in such shady operations. The schoolmaster swore in vain that God was God, that the Virgin was a virgin and that two plus two makes four—the sister wouldn't change her mind. The dead should be left to their death just as the living to their life. But she was finally brought to reason, to understand that it was a question of burying Citrouille scientifically, and she helped the learned master gather his herbs.

What happened next between the teacher, the nurse and their victim has not been recorded either in the chronicles of Flea Island nor in the archives of the mainland. The oral literature of the island merely reports that the schoolmaster with his naturalist's zeal so stuffed poor Citrouille with the plant or juice of absinthe, anemones, artichokes, asters, azaleas, beans, birch, blueberries, box tree, campanula, carrots, chard, dahlias, eggplants, fiddleheads and grass, that in a single stroke Citrouille's lungs, stomach and guts were emptied of the barrels of salt water he had drunk. After all this, Citrouille sneezed, then opened his eyes.

The nursing sister let out a great scream. In her long career of caring for old people in the nursing home, never had such a thing happened to her. But the most disconcerted was the schoolmaster. Definitely his science was finally going to get the better of him and lead him too far. When his mixture of herbs started bringing the dead back to life, things were beginning to smell of Beelzebub. And, leaving the ghost in the lurch, the two undertakers fled the enchanted island as fast as they could row.

Left alone in an empty and silent kingdom, Citrouille let his eyes wander over the yellow and blue countryside which he couldn't recognize at first. Then his pupils adjusted and he could finally distinguish his fingers from the hay and the land from water. He knew that he was coming back from a long journey somewhere—Butte du Moulin or Ruisseau des Pottes or Pointe à Jérôme—he no longer remembered clearly. Too many things were churning in his stomach, churning in his stomach, churning in his stomach. . . . Then, hitting the shore in a supreme effort to cling to the earth, the shipwrecked man gave back to the island all the silly herbs the learned naturalist had stuffed him with.

And sighing with comfort, Citrouille looked towards the

sea where Don l'Orignal's fleet was advancing with cross and candles at its head.

Chapter Twenty Three

Concerning the Flea Islanders' sudden terror which soon turned to gaiety.

The funeral procession landed on the island reciting and chanting prayers for the repose of the dead. Since the Flea nation was entirely non-Latin in origin, it was apt to confound ablatives, genitives and accusatives in a way to render the meaning of the requests it addressed to the heavens completely unintelligible to itself and Citrouille. They were vaguely aware of crying something or other from the depths of the abyss—that a watcher somewhere was hoping for Aurora; that someone held his sins before him while another trailed his works behind him; and that a sacrifice would be made of a holocaust or a helicopter, it wasn't quite clear which. *Dies illa, dies irae, quescat aeternam Domine, R.I.P.*

The cross and the two candlesticks were planted in the sand while the first six knights of the kingdom followed the officiating priest to raise the body. But here a surprise awaited them, for the body got up by itself.

The phenomenon of terror before ghostly appearances proved to be virtually universal at the time of Citrouille's resurrection. For the reactions of the Flea Islanders were identical to those of the mainlanders. All these courageous people flung the banner and candles into the sea and jumped into their boats. Even La Sainte, who had not stopped mourning her son, shouted in panic, "Citrouille, what's got into ya?"

It was La Sagouine who first sniffed out the truth.

"Could it really be," she proposed," that the servant of the Good Lord was badly drownded?"

This revelation froze the hearts of all the Flea Islanders. Then Don l'Orignal snorted, readjusted his horns and put out a still hesitant hand to the ghost come back to life. But La Sainte had beaten him this time. Instead of the loving touch of his king, Citrouille received from his mother the mightiest slap of his career as an only son.

"That'll learn ya," said his enraged mother, "to turn our hearts upside down like that."

Then, throwing herself on her son's neck, she laughed and cried all at once, muttering those abusive and naughty words that in Flea language are familiar endearments.

This highly emotional people could pass rapidly from the depths of sadness to the most terrifying fear, then to the most frenzied joy. And without taking too much offence at the extraordinary event, the lively Flea Islanders, getting what they wanted out of the miracle, frolicked and made merry in Citrouille's honour.

"Citrouille's returned!"

"The returned resurrected!"

"The resurrected resuscitated!"

"Returned, revived, returned, recaptured!"

"Rrrrr! Rrrrr!"

"Purrrr . . . rrr . . . rrrr, Citrouille!"

"The resuscitated Recitrouille!"

Poor Recitrouille, who indeed felt returned from somewhere, hadn't yet managed to piece together the fragments of the great dream that he had wanted to drown. The pieces of this shipwrecked dream were still wandering among the seaweed at the bottom of the sea, seeking Citrouille's heart again.

Stunned and stupefied, the man escaped from the sea and love stared straight ahead at the mainland beyond the horizon, where it seemed to him his memories had flown.

Meanwhile, beyond the horizon, all Citrouille's memories were being kept warm in the heart of the fair Adeline, standing silently in front of a big empty grave.

Chapter Twenty Four

Concerning Flea Island's joyous revel to celebrate Citrouille's survival.

Don l'Orignal and his people were all men of hearty constitution and sound digestion. More than anyone else in those days, these merry fellows loved to eat hearty and drink deep. And when they had done both well, they showed the greatest capacity for joy and excess ever encountered in the entire eastern part of the country.

Accordions began to pump, violins to screech, feet to beat boards and throats to bawl out all the charming nonsense that heated brains can come up with. On such days, everybody would have come to the rescue of Waterloo without hesitation, and would have willingly rebuilt the temple of Jerusalem, if they had known of its destruction.

Unable to perform on a grander scale, they went through a small production of the history of the world for the people in the pit. The scene began with La Cruche offering Michel-Archange two ravishing and tempting red apples. However, La Sagouine intervened in time to prevent Adam from yielding a second time and then they went on to Cain and Abel. These roles were played by Noume and Citrouille, the unfortunate Citrouille, of course, falling under fate's blows once again. But the hero's resurrection was commemorated in grand style by calling Abel back to life. Don l'Orignal himself played the role of the venerable Noah, leading all the rabbits, cats and fleas of the island into his ark while the bums poured buckets of water over his head. La Sainte reserved for herself the role of the pillar of salt; La Cruche was Ruth lying beside Boaz; while La Sagouine sliced off the head of Bidoche-Holofernes.

This biblical pageant took place amidst shouting matches, applause, clinking of jugs and the swaying of a crowd drunk with joy and dandelion wine.

"Whata ya think La Sagouine does when she shines a place up?"

"She rubs."

"She opens her ears wide and listens."

"When the people on land gots fleas, it's the people at sea that scratches."

"The godalmightys and bejeezuses from the island a never given in to them mainlanders."

"Make a face at them schoolboys and they just thinks ya got a crooked mug."

"Crooked or not, I got a full one."

"Hee - hee!"

"The teacher pumped water outa Citrouille's guts."

"The teacher gave us back our Citrouille sound as a drum."

"Hurray fer the schoolmaster and fer the school!"

"And we didn't even thank the blessed redeemer."

"Did anybody think about thankin the teacher?"

"Book learnin or not, the egghead's done just like the others. When he seen the dead man gettin up, he took to his heels and cleared out."

"But that didn't stop him from savin Citrouille. We oughta be thankful to him fer that."

"Of course, we's thankful!"

"Maybe we could tell him."

"Well, he ain't here."

"Maybe we could go tell him over there."

"Over there?"

"Over there. A party fer the teacher!"

"A party!"

Such were the sparks thrown off by their elegant and luminous repartee. On the spot Flea Island decided to go to town that night to surprise the courageous schoolmaster, Citrouille's saviour, with their gratitude.

Meanwhile, the schoolmaster was unaware of the invasion being plotted. Having recovered from his terror, he left his house the same evening on a nocturnal excursion to the woods in search of new herbs.

Chapter Twenty Five

Concerning the very gracious manner in which the Flea Islanders paid their debt of gratitude to the schoolmaster.

It was a moonless night. They were in luck. They had to take advantage of the brief truce in the sky before the arrival of a crowd of stars. And the hooded invaders slid their soft moccasins over the grass.

Don l'Orignal tried two doors and the trap to the cellar. Then, without a word, he pointed out to his gang the low kitchen window. And the whole party swept in.

"Shush yer traps, godalmightyhellfire! If it's sposed to be a surprise, it'll be a surprise. I'll damn well make sure of that."

And prodding each one in the back, Don l'Orignal hid his group behind chairs, tables and dressers.

Suddenly, the sound of the shattering of a window came from the direction of the kitchen. Don l'Orignal straightened his horns and the whole assembly lifted its heads from the depths of its hiding places. La Sainte immediately took charge of the investigation.

"It's La Sagouine. She's shoved her foot through the wrong window," she said. "Through the shut one."

Don l'Orignal shook his fur crown seven or eight times to let the clumsy woman see clearly that this was not the way of the world and that if they were told to go through the window, that didn't mean sticking their feet through the panes.

"It wasn't her feet," corrected Boy à Polyte. "It was her mop."

Don l'Orignal snorted, "Anyway, why's she gotta drag her mop around after her everywhere?"

La Sagouine bristled, "And who's gonna sweep up the pieces after the evenin get together?"

"Damn sure'll be pieces if we start breakin the windows," said a bum.

Don l'Orignal, who had forty years' experience in government, knew when to take and when to leave the last word, and he turned to his squire Michel-Archange who understood that he must repair the damage.

Then everybody looked hard for a pane of glass. Since her rival's clumsy move, La Sainte had felt her prestige rising. Wanting to add to her credit, she called out proudly, "I got one!"

But La Sagouine wasn't used to being displaced without a fight and she laughed derisively, "That ain't a window, that's a mirror. Ya think ya'd never seen one."

And La Sainte left it at that.

Meanwhile, Don l'Orignal ordered the bums to plug the frame with the mirror until something better could be found. And La Sainte went ahead of them into the kitchen.

La Sagouine, who felt the need to justify herself, grumbled, "It was Noume's idea anyway to give a party fer the teacher in his own house."

"We damn well couldn't entertain him in our shacks," retorted the knight. "Gotta grab the chance while . . ."

But nobody ever knew what chance was to be grabbed, for Noume's words were carried away in a tremendous shout.

"There he is!"

"Holy Mother of God!" shouted La Sagouine. "Everybody hide!"

"Hide," repeated Don l'Orignal. "When I stick my head above the chair, everybody shout surprise."

Then there was a deathly silence in the schoolmaster's house. No trace of a Flea man anywhere.

So, sticking his nose between the feet of his table or chair, each party-goer waited anxiously for the signal. It came earlier than expected from the direction of La Sagouine's chest of drawers. And the lively Flea Islanders, mistaking the mop of the noble woman for the furry crown of their leader, came out all together from behind the furniture, shouting, "Surprise!"

At the same moment, another sound of shattering glass was heard. Then the ancient and venerable face of the poet,

Pamphile, appeared in the living room where the Flea Islanders were standing close together. And at once they understood that the bard, dazzled by the shouting and the sight of his own image in the window, had shoved his fist through the pane.

"Blessed Holy Mother," shouted La Sagouine. "The mirror!"

"Bejeezus, Pamphile, everybody thought ya was the teacher."

Michel-Archange tumbled laughing to the couch which groaned under his weight.

"Me, the schoolmaster?" said Pamphile. "Well, if I'd a school I might just be able to master it."

At that moment Noume came in, his arms loaded with bottles, singing, "Yodelay - y - y!" His father signaled to him to stop and a debate began between father and son, setting in opposition the moral theories of two generations.

"What ya got there?" asked the king.

"Don't ya recognize it any more, pa? It sure ain't the first time ya seen them."

"Where'd ya dig them up?"

"On cold ice in a big white box."

"A regiferator, it's called," intervened La Sagouine.

"Them belongs to the teacher," said the father grandly. "Don't set a finger on his things."

"Aaaaw!" said the bums.

"But look here, it's just hospitality," replied the son. "A man don't drink alone, it ain't Christian. A man gives a round to his visitors. And that's us."

"Yeah . . ." said the king hesitantly, rubbing his temples. "Well, no, cause we ain't been invited. We came on our own. We ain't no visitors till he's come back."

"Oh," said La Sainte, "he could come back late. Book learnin ain't swallowed easy as a strawberry."

Others took up the thread then, until the argument was so tightly stitched that Don l'Orignal finally thought they might very well be the prospective guests of a host in absentia.

When the schoolmaster came back from the woods in the wee hours of the morning, he stopped, glued to his doorstep, open-mouthed in front of a breath-taking sight.

Flea Island was there, floating over the furniture, the floor, the landing—a scene of pillage like a wave of Tartars would have left. Then from the depths of a battered arm chair, he heard the voice of Michel-Archange.

"He's a jolly good fellow, the teacher . . . a damn good devil. Yeah . . . a bloody good devil. Any country that can make a man like the teacher. . . . Any country . . . urp! A good devil, the teacher's country . . . urp!—A hell of a good devil . . . surprise!

Chapter Twenty Six

How the terrified town organized itself after the barbarian invasion into civilized country.

The schoolmaster didn't have to take legal action. Even before sunrise, the whole town was well aware of the nocturnal expedition of the Flea Islanders. For that night nothing had escaped the watchful eye of the keeper who had followed the cunning manoeuvres of his dearest enemies from the heights of his lighthouse. "The Fleas are preparing an attack," he'd said to himself. So the mainland knew about the attack before morning.

This time the proceedings were taken care of by the barber. Rumour had it that the dear man found it difficult to swallow the astonishing success of his rival, the teacher, in the Citrouille affair. Here it must be made clear that the barber had in past years also nourished serious scientific pretensions which hadn't brought him as much happiness as he'd hoped. This secret frustration had made him the unavowed adversary of the schoolmaster, who had never noticed through his thick glasses this strange affliction which psychology might one day name the "Barber's Complex."

This barber, then, took charge of the matter. Carrying his whole arsenal of evidence in a big suitcase, he came looking for the mayor. There, in front of the cabinet, the legislature and the constituent assembly, he showed by the deductive method that the neighbouring country had landed on the mainland that night, that enemy troops had camped for several hours in a respectable house in the town, that the respectable master of this respectable house was by chance absent from the house at this same instant, and that the whole thing was beginning to smell of Judas.

The nursing sister, who had listened with growing emotion to the beautiful prose of the barber, suddenly understood that the speaker was attacking the wisdom and generosity of the schoolmaster who had brought someone half dead back to life before her very eyes. Without stopping to take the pulse of the assembly or to choose a plan, the nurse undertook the defence of the dead, the living, and the learned man who had worked so well in the service of both.

The banker had not yet said much in the struggle between the island and the mainland. For some time he had had an inkling of the total interests sleeping between water and land, interests from which a skilful hand ought to know how to extract a profit. And the financier warned the townsfolk of the dangers of an intestinal war and proposed that they busy themselves instead with their common enemy.

The mayor understood that the wisdom of the day came from the banker and, with a wave of her hand, she ordered the barber to be quiet. Then, climbing onto her rostrum, she seized the reigns of power once more and expounded her philosophy of peace to her subjects.

When they separated after the debate, the assembly had voted for conscription, coalition, conspiracy, colonization, plus a commanding war budget.

All this lasted until the cows came home, the time when on Flea Island the bums coated their strings with resin and La Cruche began her learned and scientific ambling among the cabins.

Chapter Twenty Seven

Concerning La Sagouine's plea in defence of feudal rights and the brilliant idea Citrouille gained from it.

The townsfolk of the mainland concealed their military preparations with such discretion that their designs escaped the attention of their closest and most cunning neighbours on the plain. But they did not escape the attention of the Flea Islanders.

"Them folks over there's just itchin fer somethin," declared Sir Noume one day.

"Well, let em scratch," replied La Sainte.

Flea Island made a circle around the messenger to hear his secret.

Then Noume expounded to his royal father and his noble subjects on the recent discoveries of Soldat-Bidoche in the lighthouse tower. Something fishy was happening there, something that stank. Arms and munitions were being piled up and the keeper had traced a map of the island on the wall with a compass.

"Sons of bitches!" shouted La Sagouine, while her husband, Michel-Archange, who felt his hot general's blood tickling his veins, rubbed his hands.

"Let em come, bejeezus! We wouldn't sell em three clovers."

"Oh, if that's all, they could take it away from us without buyin," replied Don l'Orignal calmly. "The island don't belong to nobody."

"How's that, nobody?" Noume bridled. "Didn't ya get yer land from yer late father?"

"Yeah, but my late father didn't pay very much fer it," said the king. "One fine evenin when he'd taken a wife, he needed a place to stretch out, so he set up his shack in the hay at the water's edge where nobody'd drive him out that night. We's still here."

Don l'Orignal cracked his fingers while his left eye searched the sea for a firm little spot to rest on. Then he added thoughtfully, "Land never belongs to nobody."

Hearing these words, La Sagouine leaped up from her throne of 'mashkoui' and struck the air three times with her clenched fist. Then, wrinkling her nose and mouth into a grimace that always announced deep and audacious thoughts, she hurled forth, "Jos and Pit and Boy and Thomas Picoté Viens-que-je-t'arrache all lived on this here land before my man and me. And our descendants come into the world on the land of their ancestors."

"But the ancestors," continued Don l'Orignal, "didn't pay nothin fer the land either."

"Nothin, eh?" bristled La Sagouine. "My father, Jos à Pit, paid em a keg of home-brew that he made himself in a cellar dug with his own two hands. There! His father, Pit à Boy, paid em smelts and oysters every one of God's winters, hot or cold. And his late grandfather, Boy à Thomas Picoté, paid them bastards that dared tell him the land wasn't his with kicks in the ass. That's how the bit of land come to us from Thomas Picoté to Boy to Pit to Jos to me, La Sagouine. And I'll leave it to our descendants on my deceased death."

"We'll drink a tea deum to celebrate that," guffawed a bum, drawing a dismal wail from his accordion.

The island's proceedings took place around Don l'Orignal's stump in the middle of the country. All the Flea Islanders were there, shouting loudly, gesticulating a lot, and spitting copiously. La Sagouine, who as usual had the inside track, didn't give way to anybody. And the debate advanced from the pro to the con, from right to left, from the obvious to the obscure, from revolt to revolution.

While his native land was engaged in this debate to affirm its rights and rediscover its identity, Citrouille, survivor of the ocean depths, was dreaming all by himself. One sentence of La Sagouine's had just cut a clear path through the thick hair in his ear and stealthily approached his brain. "That's how the bit of land come to us," she had said. And Don l'Orignal had asserted that land belonged to nobody.

"The land ain't nobody's but comes to them that knows how to grab it, settle there and make themselves master," thought Citrouille. And for the first time since his failed death, he smiled softly at the night.

Chapter Twenty Eight

How the keeper came close to capturing the biggest quarry of his life.

The lighthouse keeper was at his post. Future generations could never reproach him for having failed to be a vigilant sentinel that day. Confronted with the extraordinary event taking place below, on water and land, he carried out his duty with decisiveness, precision, promptness and integrity.

Since daybreak the irreproachable keeper had been in his tower—alert, nervous, watchful—joyfully and zealously fulfilling his purpose in the world. Then he picked up the first message. Oh, as yet a faint warning to which anyone but he would have paid no attention. But vigilance and curiosity are the very vocation of a lighthouse keeper, to whom nothing is neutral or commonplace. He knows that a sneeze often hides a neurosis and an accidental trough in the sea may cover an invader.

That morning the sea sneezed. The first signal the keeper received came in the guise of a rare fish. Was it a sea-cow? A porpoise? A dolphin? The keeper lost no time in unnecessary conjecture. He doubled the power of the light. It was a man.

The most marvellous hunt of the keeper's life began then. All his lights concentrated their beams on the quarry that offered itself floundering in the waves and light. The fearless hunter drooled with joy. This game at least wouldn't get away, even if he had to give half his soul for it.

He gave his whole soul.

But let's not get ahead of ourselves. At the hour of the serious events related in this very true story, the keeper had all his soul, all his heart, all his mind ready to cast off and close the trap on the poor swimmer who was desperately trying to reach shore.

When the keeper was sure of the precise point where the

landing would take place, he turned out the lights, enjoined silence on his tower and camouflaged his field glass under a pile of leaves. Then he followed the intruder, who was now in the shadow of the cliff threading his way among rocks rounded by the sea over the centuries. He lost him, found him again, then lost him once more. A few seconds later, he spotted him at the entrance to a cave where he was in the process of fixing six planks onto four tires. And he understood.

In a sudden flash the keeper understood everything. The invader came from Flea Island, his name was Citrouille, he had swum across the channel and he was building a raft for the return trip.

"Therefore, our man is not going to leave alone," the excited keeper concluded, using the most rigorous logic.

And he licked his lips sensuously.

The alarm must be given immediately. . . . No, no alert. Subtle work, strategy, the hunter's science. Seize the quarry in the act, crush his paws and knife him. But first of all, warn the mayor.

Now here awaited the most terrible disappointment ever inflicted on a keeper. The mayor, his rightful sovereign, to whom he offered with all the zeal of a sworn keeper the rarest bouquet of her career, listened to his report without flinching, without wincing, without showing the slightest shadow of anger. She contented herself with giving him a very enigmatic order, while squinting in the direction of the nunnery.

"Make sure nobody puts any obstacles in the way of his comings and goings or his departure."

The keeper stammered,' nonplussed, "Not even if he leaves with one of our girls?"

"Not even then," insisted the mayor, drumming her fingers on her starched collar.

And, without tearing her eyes from the sea whose huge waves rolled right to the base of the nunnery, she dismissed the lighthouse keeper with a flick of her fingers.

The keeper counted as he climbed back up the one hundred and thirty-two steps of his tower. Once again the Fleas had eluded him, the mystery of his mistress had eluded him and his own soul had eluded him. Attacking the maps of the island he had so carefully drawn, he made a torch of them.

"Bejeezus godalmightyhellfire!" he spat out from the top of his tower, unaware that he was the first of the mainlanders to plagiarize the Flea Islanders. "Let the devil take me!"

That day the devil really had too much to do. Over by the town hall, he was very busy assembling the general staff of the townsfolk who were congratulating themselves on the magnificent opportunity that fortune had offered them to win a final victory over their worst enemy. Clumsy Citrouille who was carrying away on his raft the most celebrated beauty of the mainland couldn't suspect the service he was doing for his opponents hiding behind their shutters.

But, in fact, had clumsy Citrouille known that the highest masters and civil servants of the state were spying on his every movement, that the mayor was plotting her worst revenge and that Flea Island would be made to pay dearly for this kidnapping, he could not for a single second have torn his eyes away from the smile directed only at him, at Citrouille alone. For as far as he was concerned, the rest of the world had sunk forever to the bottom of the sea.

Chapter Twenty Nine

How the news of the kidnapping of Adeline spread throughout the town and what revenge the milliner endeavoured to derive from it.

The mayor and her staff let Citrouille get a head start. Then they informed the town. At once the merchant—who to his great surprise had not been summoned to the town hall that day—cried aloud. In less than an hour the entire population had been alerted. Adeline had been abducted again, the pearl of the mainland kidnapped. And all the old people of the country wailed a lament, while the young howled in revolt.

Decidedly the gods favoured the sovereign's plans. Everything came together as she had foreseen, producing in her people the hoped-for effect. And the mayor relished the thought of her sway over men, things and fate.

When she felt the townspeople sufficiently ripe for anger, she called an extraordinary session of parliament and launched a plebiscite. The mayor appealed to the people: yes or no, do you agree to the destruction of the little island of hay and fleas? And, if yes, would they accord her and her lieutenants complete power to act in this difficult and delicate matter?

The material organization of the plebiscite was entrusted to the barber and the milliner who divided up the town, the left bank coming to the clever man, the right to the deserving and respectable lady of the millinery shop. In each house, ballots were distributed along with copious literature about modern democracies, the defence of the family, the preparation for marriage, the protection of animals, the blessings of sobriety, the art of public speaking and aid to underdeveloped countries. All this was gone over and added to by the barber's eloquence and the milliner's living example.

However, during the conspiracy, a small incident occurred which almost compromised the success of the plebiscite and which taught the mayor that you can't make an omelette without breaking eggs, that a man is judged by his work, a tree is known by its fruit, the cask savours of the first wine, and wolves sometimes eat each other. This tree, this cask, this wolf, was the milliner.

This milliner, who was absolute master of all the hats in town (and consequently arbitrated women's fashion), by an unjust caprice of nature had never managed to take advantage of this fashion, source of the elegance and charm of the wives of the town's solid citizens. None of the hats worn on the most ravishing heads of the country had ever stayed more than five minutes on her own rebellious and unmanageable locks. As a result, the milliner had always had it in for all women, especially for the most elegant and beautiful.

At the head of this list were the fair Adeline and the elegant mayor. So the milliner, not forgiving these two women for their heads, had sworn to set them against each other. Now her two rivals themselves gave her the opportunity. Adeline's disloyalty to her country, that led to the mayor's treachery towards Adeline, prompted the milliner's felony to both Adeline and the mayor.

The milliner went off to find the merchant and spoke to him quietly for a minute. Then she withdrew before the explosion.

"What!" the unhappy father suddenly leaped up, grasping the double dealing of the general staff.

So he had been betrayed! So his daughter had served as bait! And he, the merchant, would serve as a lesson for the whole village! And, forgetting to close his shop for the first time, the merchant marched on the town hall, determined to overthrow the government if necessary.

The mayor had great difficulty calming him. It even cost her a bribe, for which she was long in forgiving the milliner. The town, nevertheless, accorded complete authority to the mayor and her council to send troops to the island, to capture or destroy it according to the moon, the winds, or the greatest good of all.

Chapter Thirty

How a holy hermit of the seas set the Flea Islanders on the trail of their brave lost hero.

That morning, Flea Island bathed in a sea tickled by the boldest sun ever seen since the famous year of the bed bugs. A whole generation had elapsed since that impromptu landing of foreigners which had displaced the first occupants from their ancestral fiefs in a few days. But these fleas, with the aid of the Flea people, had finally triumphed over the intruder and peace had come again to the island.

"The morning of the bed bugs was a morning like today," uttered the poet Pamphile with a prophetic air. "Is it gonna be lice this time?"

But the Flea Islanders swore fidelity once more to the fleas and promised to trounce any species of upstart insect that dared compete against them.

"When ya got fleas ya ain't got lice," declared La Sainte reflectively, scratching her head.

And all of Flea Island agreed, sticking out their tongues at the mainland.

These broad grins missed their target, however. It was a holy hermit who collected them while beaching his little birch-bark canoe on the south shore of the island. The abashed Flea people changed their minds very quickly, however, and approached the strange, thin, bearded figure who seemed to be looking for somebody.

Don l'Orignal did the honours for the island. He offered the hermit of the seas the first stump on his right and a pinch of tobacco. The saintly man graciously accepted this hospitality and proved it to the whole island by hitting the royal spittoon on the first try from a distance of more than four feet. This prowess, which placed the hermit among the most worthy of the old men at court, won him the keys to the island and enabled him to accomplish the mission that had drawn him from his retreat.

"I met one of yer men," the hermit began.

And the island grew silent.

"He was comin on a tiny raft with a dame, a gorgeous creature. They looked a lot like the first couple to come from their Creator's hands."

The island kept quiet. Only La Sainte raised an eyebrow.

"They were comin like that straight towards me and I understood what they wanted. And it's done. I married them on the high seas."

"Hurrah - ah - ah - ah!" shouted Noume who triggered off a thunderstorm of yelling and clapping loud enough to uproot the island.

Had Citrouille himself been there, he could not have received a better welcome. And it was decided on the spot to celebrate Citrouille's wedding.

"Curse the luck! We need the bride and groom fer that," intervened Boy à Polyte who was dying to go to sea.

And the wedding party set off in search of the married couple. All day long they scoured the four seas surrounding Flea Island and, towards evening, they found Citrouille and Adeline, well and truly married, on a little island of spruce which rocked gently in the hollows of the waves.

The Flea people spent the day on Citrouille's island feasting, carousing, frolicking, building with their hands a hut of fir and thatch, flanked by a magnificent fireplace of field stone.

"Ya'll a got it, Citrouille, yer house and fireplace," the king of Flea Island said to him joyously.

And Citrouille gazed at the tower of stone that formed a throne on the centre of his island, against which leaned a frail cabin of fir.

"Well! Well!" said the young prince, rubbing his neck.

And he ordered a round of fistfuls of raspberries and chokecherries to be served.

Towards evening, as Don l'Orignal gathered together his people drunk with wild fruit, gentle wind and good living, Pamphile remembered the morning's peculiar sun and frowned.

"Hope we ain't got a plague of lice from Egypt this time," he said soberly.

Don l'Orignal quickly pushed the Flea Islanders into the boats and gave the order to depart.

The boisterous youth of Flea Island sang merry, irreverent goodbyes to the masters of the new island, watching the sun sink behind the trim fireplace of field stone. Meanwhile, their king stared straight ahead, letting out all the sails in his eagerness to reach the island before the lice.

Chapter Thirty One

Wherein the author of this so true, so veritable, so veracious tale reveals his sources and exposes his methods in order to prove his complete objectivity.

The tale of the final battle waged on Flea Island appears in no chronicle, no archives, nor in any part of the Pamphilian memoirs. And, curiously, in the national annals of the mainland no torn page is to be found for that date when, according to all conjectures, these lamentable events took place. Therefore this historical campaign has simply been wrapped in silence for reasons I cannot fathom.

In order to tell you the rest of the History of the Fleas, I have only been able to refer to secondary sources and auxiliary sciences such as archeology, numismatics, heraldry, epigraphy and sigillaria, and these disciplines have indeed provided me with an abundance of documents. In this way, beginning with five holes of a button collected many years afterward on the charred sand of the island, I was able to reconstitute the complete button, deduce from this button the shape of the buttonhole, then the sort of material in which this buttonhole had been cut, and so on until I reconstituted the complete costume which could only belong to the barber—the only one, moreover, who wore buttons with five holes.

A reader thus informed about all the care a historian takes to gather together the sparse pieces from a past buried in memories and sands, can only bow before such an effort at objectivity. This reader, nevertheless, might yet have doubts about the chronicler's impartiality, for he might interpret real facts erroneously.

In order to meet this objection, I will tell you immediately that a paternal grandmother of the said chronicler was the daughter-in-law of a third cousin of the godfather of a lateral descendant of the great-grandson of a Flea man, and that after this confession, he has no intention of denying his ancestry. However, if all this isn't enough for you, I shall add that the younger son of an aunt by marriage of the son-in-law of the grandmother of a first cousin of the Fleas was a friend of the family when he was a child. At that time, he had more than one opportunity to show his interest in this nation.

After that, I am counting on the confidence and good will of the reader, who will gladly read the rest of this controversial story into which the author has put his soul, his fortune and the name he bears.

Chapter Thirty Two

Wherein is told how a little island resisted all night and in the morning was devoured.

It was twilight that day when the townspeople took to their ships. Everything had gone according to the mayor's expectations. Citrouille's disappearance had roused Flea Island which at once dashed off on his heels, emptying the island of everybody who could still walk, sail and go on a binge. Thus deserted, the land of hay and fleas remained defenceless, facing an invader who was stoutly booted, helmeted, gloved and armed with heavy artillery. Such a little island confronted by such a superb enemy could only bend, curl up, go down by the bows and sink. That's what the mayor figured when, at the head of her troops, she came alongside the shores of Flea Island.

Huge, immobile, sitting on its hindquarters, the town's fleet was there, looking at the little yellow island and savouring it in advance. Since it knew very well that it would eat the island, the fleet was in no hurry, though when the island took its head out of the water, the boats began to laugh wickedly.

"Ho, ho, little island of fleas," a boat waggled its big red flag like the tongue of a famished wolf.

The island sensed it was lost. . . . One moment, remembering the story of Mr. Seguin's goat (which had fought all night only to be eaten in the morning), the island told itself it would be better to be eaten at once. Then, thinking better of this, it fell into a watchful position, head low with its beautiful dunes in the shape of two horns held up against the sea like the brave little island of fleas that it was . . .

Not that it had any hope of sinking the ships—fleas

don't win victories over boats—but simply to see if it could hold out as long as Mr. Seguin's goat.

Then the monstrous fleet advanced and the little dunes, the long hay and the agile fleas joined the dance.

Oh, the courageous little island! How it put its heart into it! More than ten times (I'm not lying) it pushed the boats against the reefs, assailed them with huge breakers, made them run aground on its sands. During truces, the faithful island looked questioningly at the horizon to see if its masters would not come running to its aid. Then it returned to the fight with a spirit full of courage. . . . This lasted all night. From time to time the little island looked at the stars dancing in the clear sky and said to itself, "Oh! If only I can last till dawn . . ."

One after another the stars went out. Flea Island increased the blows from its dunes and gusts of wind, while the fleet redoubled its oar strokes. . . . A pale ray of light appeared on the horizon. . . . With the sun coming out of the sea returned Don l'Orignal's fleet.

"At last!" said the poor island, who was only waiting for the return of its masters to die. And out into the sea it stretched its long golden hay that was burning.

The townspeople's fleet fell upon the little island and ate it up.

And then, in the morning, the wolf ate up Mr. Seguin's goat.

Chapter Thirty Three

Concerning La Sagouine's lamentations on the destruction of her island.

Don l'Orignal's fleet tossed happily on the southern sea coming back from the dauntless Citrouille's wedding. The Flea Islanders laughed and shouted, heedless of the weather, the world, and eternal life. Only the present counted for them, filled with forgotten memories and bearing an unknown future. They were coming along on the sea, straight towards the island that was their pride and joy.

And it was an island in flames floating on the water that caught their eye.

In a minute all the sails and oars were frozen. The fleet of the Flea nation came to a halt on the sea and Don l'Orignal, horns on his head, stood up in the prow of his schooner.

"Godalmightyhellfire! Our fleas is burnin," he shouted, while raising his spruce sceptre to the sky.

At once the boats and punts shuddered and the oars struck the southern sea with such a blow that the ocean trembled.

"Fire! Fire!" shouted the bowsprits and the shrouds.

But it was too late. The little island had waited all night long for its masters and couldn't resist a minute longer. Hay and undisciplined fleas faced with a thirsty and resolute wall of flames, you understand! However, the brave little island didn't want to die without letting its masters see the courage and talent which it had shown that night. And, before being extinguished, it gave a last thrust with its dunes, sending three big red flames back into the sea which swallowed them up at once. After this, Flea Island rose no more.

Don l'Orignal's heart was too swollen to recite the

lament for his beloved island. It was La Sagouine, strong woman in trying circumstances, who performed this ritual.

Sitting on the side of her punt she wept in remembrance of you, o Flea Island! She hung her woollen shawl on the single mast of her boat.

"How can anybody keep quiet," she said, "when she sees an island in ashes? If ever I forget ya, let my tongue stick to the roof of my mouth, to my throat and my guts! What can I say to ya? Is there anybody like ya, Flea Island? That I can compare ya to, to make ya feel better, little island of yellow hay? Fer yer wound was as wide as the ocean."

Then, turning to the mainland, she raised her right arm and roared loudly enough to be heard by the whole continent.

"Woe to ya, whitewashed city of rotten people! Woe to ya fine men, lettin widows and orphans die sooner than buy their cod that stinks of fisherman's sweat! Woe to ya skinflints who don't wanna marry yer daughters to our guys so yer blood'll stay pale and ya'll look like Holy Jesus of Prague! Woe to ya sons of bitches who burns our islands so as to wash yer eyeballs cause ya don't wanna look at the shacks of us poor folk! Woe to ya others, ya church mice, ya Tartuffes, ya Holier-than-Thous, ya toads in holy water who deported us from our land so ya could clear yer conscience that's tired of puttin up with us and our dirty feet and rottin teeth! But listen closely to me, La Sagouine, daughter of Jos à Pit à Boy à Thomas Picoté, who's talkin to ya. There'll come a day when ya'll crawl on all fours, pickin up the shit ya flung at us and that day ya'll know the bomination of desolation, I prophesy that fer ya."

Running out of breath, the valiant woman let fall her arm which beseeched heaven to judge between the mainland and her island, and she fell silent. One by one the Flea people set foot on the blackened sand and walked softly to their shacks, avoiding stepping on the charred hay and fleas.

Chapter Thirty Four

Concerning the life that went on smoothly on the mainland while they forgot that one day a little island had risen out of the sea.

Along the shores of my country, right beside yours, the tranquil and honourable life of the worthy people of the mainland had begun its peaceful course again. Sweetly, innocently, the springs had begun to sing again, the fields to flower, the men to plant, hoe, produce and market, as if the sea had never thrown a wretched island at their heads one fine morning.

Moreover, this wretched island was very calmly forgotten. It floated all alone on the open sea, adrift like a felled oak. The northeaster and the southwester fought over it the way children play with a balloon. And the little island, having lost its long hay and its pretty dunes, was tossed about by the fierce winds and waves, no longer daring to show the sun its completely blackened back and its broken paws.

Thus it was that the island finally passed out of sight of the mainland and consequently passed out of its history and customs. Flea Island didn't even pass into legend, didn't carve a tiny niche for itself in the mainland's folklore, because the day after the fight the continent had forgotten everything.

One evening, however, the keeper was watching alone at his lighthouse. And without understanding yet what had come over him, he slipped his hand under his shirt and began scratching. Then, suddenly, he remembered. A long time ago, oh, almost in prehistoric times, he had made the same gesture without thinking. What strange thing was happening to him?

And the keeper began to go down the one hundred and

thirty-two steps of his lighthouse, trying there to recapture the memory that was simmering in his loins by taking backwards each step that he had made on the first day of the incredible adventure. And in this way he came to the fleas.

The fleas!

This time, he remembered clearly. The fleas . . . the island . . . Don l'Orignal's people. And again the keeper scratched himself. Over his whole body he felt that strange itching that had come over him every time he levelled his searchlight on the extraordinary kingdom born of the fleas. Panic-stricken, he climbed again to the top of his tower and played his four powerful beams on the four points of the compass.

The poor keeper was making too much of it. He didn't need all his artillery to discover the new vision presented to his eyes and confused mind. For the scene that suddenly caught at this throat was taking place right at his feet, at the foot of the lighthouse, at a distance visible to the naked eye.

At the end of his spyglass the keeper caught sight of the big, bearded and horned figure of Don l'Orignal, showing all his teeth as he smiled, surrounded by his people who were in the process of building shacks and digging wells.

Epilogue

Many years after the glorious events related in this tale, one of the direct ancestors of a cousin of mine told the rest of the story of the Fleas as he had witnessed it.

He told how he had passed through the town where our mayor had made rain and sunshine for over a quarter of a century, and he was very surprised not to find her in the town hall. Making his way then to the barber shop, the general store, the millinery shop, the hospital, the school and the bank, he was stunned by the great silence in what had formerly been the busiest districts of the town.

Everything in the village was topsy turvy. The bank bore a sign saying, "We love our children"; on the school was written "A good investment"; in front of the old people's home a red, white and blue pole sat in honour; and on the barber shop could be read "Silence, sick are resting." Everywhere the almost deserted streets presented the curious sight of a town asleep for a hundred years.

What had happened to the town so well established on the firm soil of the mainland along the shores of my country? My cousin's ancestor continued to walk through the village and reached the area by the lighthouse. And there he understood.

He understood that the town had been slightly displaced, that the population in future would be concentrated lower down, close to the water, that this population moreover had been renewed . . . completely renewed. He didn't recognize the famous mayor who had made a whole continent tremble, but in her place reigned a squealing gossip who continually pushed an arsenal of mops, buckets and dust rags in front of her. He could not find the milliner any more, but instead a sort of modest ascetic by the name of La Sainte who put herself through the worst contortions to prove that she hadn't usurped her name. Similarly, he looked in vain for the barber, the banker, the merchant and the schoolmaster. This entire elite had given way to a tribe of hairy and bearded creatures, spitting thick and fast and swearing by all the devils in hell. And in the midst of this developing nation stood the royal tent, topped by the horns of a moose, bearings of the first dynasty.

My cousin's ancestor continued his investigation on the mainland and discovered the strange destiny of that civilized people of high culture and strong tradition. Not long after the settlement of the Flea people at the foot of the lighthouse, the keeper had disappeared. For a time it was believed that the tide had swallowed him up or that the fleas had eaten him. But soon it was learned that, overwhelmed by the geometrical progression of the inferior species sprouting up around his lighthouse, he had quite simply left the place. Without warning, he had left by sea one evening and had sailed for a long time before landing on a small floating island.

When the townsfolk had been informed about the keeper's place of exile and the conditions of life there, they left one after the other and landed on the little island, all of them, without consultation. In the beginning, they came there to build summer cottages and spend their holidays. But little by little, time erased from their memories the traces of those fat years and of civilization.

Without really knowing at what moment the transformation had taken place, they gradually gave up their top hats and starched collars and dressed less formally. They also stopped cultivating the art of sauces and hors d'oeuvres, and lived off the island's produce. Similarly, their summer cottages were equipped with stove pipes and covered with shingles to protect them from the cold when the island's new inhabitants decided to spend the winter there.

Like any evolution, that of the people from the mainland, turned islanders, was slow and painful. It was not without difficulty that they learned to do without luxuries and cliques. It was only after several generations that this civilized nation managed to erase from its customs its old habits, morals and culture. It must be said that in this matter Flea Island helped them.

For in time, the stout little island had tidied itself up, wiped its face and let its roots and long hay grow again. And with the hay, the fleas reappeared. So after a few generations, the people of the mainland had turned into Flea Islanders.

While on New Flea Island the former townsfolk were turning into Flea people, on the mainland the former Flea people were slowly becoming respectably bourgeois. One fine day, La Sagouine crossed the market square turning up a proud stiff collar of lace. The next day, La Sainte covered her long arms in long gloves and rolled her long fingers around a silk purse. All the Flea women immediately emulated these fashions, emptying the milliner's old store in two days.

Little by little, the barbarians penetrated the mysteries of civilization. They discovered bridge, corsets, plum pudding, mushroom sauce, table manners, religious protocol, social hierarchy and diplomatic and ministerial power play. And then the royal lineage of Don l'Orignal might be seen climbing onto a keg of nails to thump his tub at election time.

Slowly the world was changing, upsetting class structure, civilizing the barbarians and barbarizing the urbane. All this was the fault of a little island of hay and fleas that one day had risen with the sun from the sea.

Then over there, far away, another island tossed about on the trough of the waves—a tiny island of green firs alive with a new people, born of Adeline and Citrouille. The tribe of Citrouilles cultivated and exploited its island, a hardy and vigorous developing world. Every morning the young Citrouilles looked proudly ahead at the infinite sheet of water and the future. But in the evenings, sometimes, they gazed at the sun setting over the old world and said with a sort of nostalgia, "Godalmightyhellfire, just the same . . ."

The End